Christmas at Manoria

Also by Jane Shoup

Down in the Valley
Spirit of the Valley
Will of the Valley
Knightfall
The Restoration
Zan, Birth of a Legend
The Key
A Choice of Captors
Ammey McKeaf, Book 1~ The Chronicles of Azulland
Heirs to the Throne, Book 2 ~ Chronicles of Azulland
Into Shadow, Book 3 ~ The Chronicles of Azulland
Charity Cases
Santa:2020 The Final Ride
The Time Tunnel of August Kaplan
An American Baroness, Book 1~ Sons of Barons
Nearly a Marquess, Book 2 ~ Sons of Barons
London's Adonis, Book 3 ~ Sons of Barons

Copyright © 2023 by Jane Shoup
ISBN: 978-1-7351648-8-5

.

Dear Reader,

Christmas at Manoria is a continuation of the lives and stories shared in books one through three of the Sons of Barons series. Naturally, that presented a challenge when considering a reader who might pick up book four first. I feared a reader getting cross-eyed as they read. (Wait … there are how many characters? Which one is this?)

I recommend readers begin with book one, of course, but I also hope each book can stand on its own. Below is a blurb on each of the books in the series. Whether you have journeyed with me from the beginning or just picked up one of my books for the first time, I hope you enjoy *Christmas at Manoria!*

Best wishes,

Jane

An American Baroness: (Book One) Alice and Jocelyn Weatherly have longed to experience their father's native London. In the spring of 1820, they get the opportunity and in time for the Season! Unbeknownst to them, their father is in league with a nobleman, Lord Merton. Their plan is a match between their children, and the trade is simple, a title for Alice in exchange for an influx of capital to pay off Merton's gambling debts.

For Nigel Walston, the future baron of Merton, family obligation is everything, but he resents having an arranged marriage foisted upon him … until he meets Alice, a beauty with two different colored eyes, a sharp mind and a fiery spirit.

In Alice's opinion, love and business should never mix, which does not mean she dislikes Nigel Walston. He is handsome, considerate, protective, and he makes her yearn in ways she did not know she was capable of. If only their fathers had not made them into a business transaction!

Nearly a Marquess: (Book Two) Twin brothers Joel and Jonathan Stewart have always enjoyed a strong bond. Joel, the elder by eight minutes, inherited the baronage, and then is unexpectedly awarded a marquisate. Amidst a culture that tends to revere the title more than the man, it is a strange experience to have one's identity and status altered.

Jane Lloyd is a widow and the mother of a young son. As the eldest daughter of an earl, she could have easily married a peer of the realm but, at eighteen years of age, she followed her heart and chose a commoner, a soldier, who soon perished in the war. In her grief, she shut herself off from society for years but, as a new season begins, one her younger sister intends on dominating, Jane feels a restlessness and a desire to join the festivities of the ton. Sadly, in her absence, she's been virtually forgotten.

When Joel and Jane meet, there is a profound and immediate chemistry between them, but nothing is simple when many would betray a friend or a sibling in order to get ahead.

London's Adonis (Book Three) Dabney Adams, frequently called *London's Adonis* in the papers, is as enigmatic as he is jaw-droppingly handsome. Not even his closest friends know what caused an estrangement with his family. As the 1821 Season draws to a close, most of those friends have found love and happiness. Unfortunately, Dab knows he is not cut from the same cloth. He's probably not even capable of fully trusting a woman, much less falling in love. Still, there should be no reason he shouldn't marry an heiress and simply move on with his life. Circumstances change when he learns his father is dying. Dab must either choose to forgive the mistakes of the past or live with the consequences.

Theodora Martel has known little but tragedy in the last year, and now her half-brother is selling the family home and forcing an unwanted marriage on her. When she is unexpectedly thrust in Dab's path, he feels an overwhelming and uncharacteristic desire to come to her rescue. Theo is unlike any lady he has ever encountered. She is fresh and brave and lovely. She makes him want to be a better man.

Only months before, he wished he could feel more … and then came Theo.

Chapter One

November 19th, 1821

On an overcast Monday morning, Hugh Pritchett strode through the campus of Christ College mentally preparing for his classes. Not the material, he knew that well. He taught history of the late Middle Ages, a subject of great interest to him. Last week, they had focused on Northern Europe and covered the Hanseatic League, an influential confederation of merchant guilds considered to be one of the most successful trade alliances in history, powerful enough to ensure the Renaissance arrived in northern Germany long before the rest of Europe.

Today's topic was the 'lady king' Margaret I, the eventual regent of Denmark, Norway and Sweden, also known as the Kalmar Union. The story of the queen's rise and reign was interesting – which did not mean that all his students would be interested. There were those among them far more intent on demonstrating their own wit through commentary than learning a damn thing. Smart alecks who hailed from families of wealth and prestige and who had been taught they could get away with most anything. The biggest offender in his first class was Royden Cimarron. The shame of it was that the twenty-year-old was intelligent, attractive, and well-spoken. He could have easily been a leader of far more than a group of mean-spirited adherents. They were bullies, the lot of them.

It was one thing when they were being disruptive in order to put on a show, it was quite another when it involved harassing another student. On Thursday last, their target had been a young man by the name of David Burr. Hugh had put a stop to it by dismissing Royden from the class for the day. In fact, he'd said Royden could stay away until he could behave in a decent, considerate manner. The authority to expel a student was probably not his to wield, but he'd done it anyway.

Royden showed up for class the following morning. He'd been uncharacteristically quiet and respectful, seemingly disappointing his followers. If that came as a surprise, Hugh was in for a bigger one when he encountered Royden as he left campus that afternoon. The young man had been waiting for him to invite him for a drink. Hugh had no desire to do so, but he was polite about it, explaining he had plans.

It would be interesting to see what today brought.

Hugh noticed a colleague, Edward Lawton, headed toward him, his robe flapping behind him. Lawton was one of the few professors that deigned to speak with him since Hugh was there on a trial basis for the Michaelmas term. Initially, Hugh had hoped the appointment would become permanent, but now he wasn't so certain. Teaching had not been as fulfilling as he'd expected it to be.

"Did you hear yet?" Lawton asked grimly when he reached him.

Hugh observed how many students loitered about. There was a definite strain in the air. "I've just arrived. What is it?"

"Your favorite student, Cimarron, killed himself."

Hugh's jaw went lax. "What?" he breathed.

Lawton nodded. "Shot and killed himself. He wasn't my favorite either," Lawton added quietly. "But it's stunned everyone. Classes have been canceled for the day."

"When was this?" Hugh stammered.

"Friday night. On the green."

Hugh swallowed, suddenly feeling unwell. Friday night. On the green. That would have been after he'd spoken with him and declined to have a drink. *Dear God.* Might he have made a difference if only he'd given the younger man a bit of his time?

"His eminence wants to see you," Lawton added.

Hugh blinked. "The dean?"

Lawton nodded. "Rumor is, the lad left three letters behind. One of them to you."

"Me?" Hugh exclaimed. "Why would he? I didn't know him well. I've had him in class this term, but—" Hugh looked around and saw how much attention was focused on him. Why would Royden have left a letter for him?

Lawton shrugged. "The young man was troubled, and he was a troublemaker. I suppose those always go hand in hand. Still...it is sad to see a life cut short like that. Such a waste." Lawton looked around. "Let me know what it's all about, will you?"

Hugh gave a noncommittal nod and walked on, feeling queasy. Royden Cimmaron may very well have been troubled and a troublemaker and a nuisance in class, but he'd been so very alive. And now he was dead? By his own hand? Hugh kept his eyes on the path in front of him as he made his way to the dean's office.

~~~

An hour and a half later, Hugh slipped into the backdoor of his families' home and found it perfectly quiet. Thankfully, he thought wryly as he headed upstairs for his room.

"Is that you, dear?" his mother called from the kitchen.

Hugh inwardly groaned. "It's me, Mother," he replied. He heaved a silent sigh as he heard her approaching.

She appeared with a dishtowel in her hands and a spotless apron over her dress looking puzzled. "Why are you here this time of day?"

"Classes were canceled. I found out when I got there."

"Why were they canceled?"

"Because of an incident," he said reluctantly. "A student...took his own life."

She gasped. "Oh, how dreadful!"

His foot was poised on the first stair, his hand on the banister. A clean getaway would have been so nice.

"Was it someone you knew?"

3

He nodded. "I can't say I knew him well, but I did know him."

She made a breathy utterance of sympathy.

"Will you excuse me? I think I'll have a short lie down."

"Of course. Are you alright?"

"Shocked," he admitted. "I feel sickened by the thing."

"Naturally," she commiserated.

He turned to fully face her, needing to acknowledge something out loud. "I can't help but wonder how much I misread him. I wish I'd tried harder to understand him."

She canted her head, her face a mask of empathy.

"I had him in class on Friday. I saw him again that afternoon and he invited me for a drink, which I declined. And then on Friday evening—"

She looked pained. "Oh, dearest," she said softly. "Of course, it's shocking. It's terrible. So often, we can never truly know what's in someone's heart and mind. They can put on such a good front. But I know you. You would have helped had you believed he needed it."

He was grateful she'd said so. It was true, wasn't it? He hadn't given that much thought about what Royden wanted, but he'd never thought the younger man to be in the depths of despair.

"Shall I bring you some tea?"

"No, thank you. I'll have some later." She nodded, and he headed upstairs. In his room, he closed the door and leaned against it. After a moment, he extracted the letter from his inner jacket pocket and went to put it in the top drawer of his chest before peering into the mirror mounted atop it. The man that stared back was nothing special, he never had been, but he'd never felt quite so substandard before. Hugh heaved a heavy sigh, removed his spectacles, and pinched the bridge of his nose. He'd had high hopes for his job, but it hadn't been what he expected. He had felt unable to reach most of his students most of the time. Now his employment had been terminated. He'd been let go.

Blamed.

Or was that too harsh? The Dean had seemed compassionate as he explained that it would be best for everyone involved if they replaced him, effective immediately. Not that anything was his fault. It wasn't. Nothing was or would be held against him. "You're not being sacked," the dean stated. "I would think it was a … mutual understanding," he said, finishing weakly. "After such a dreadful tragedy."

"If that's what you think best," Hugh replied. Had he stammered when he said it? "I would never leave anyone in a lurch."

"No, of course not. I know you wouldn't. However, the professor who retired is willing to return and finish out the term."

It was all decided and arranged, then. It was a done thing.

"I am so deeply regretful for the matter," the dean added.

"So am I," Hugh replied earnestly.

"It's simply that the student's father, Lord Olanders, is an influential man. And not at all hesitant to use that influence," he added meaningfully.

Meaning Lord Olanders wanted him gone. The man blamed him. Hugh looked down at the letter in his hand. It was not sealed. He harbored little doubt that it had been read, although he hadn't yet had a chance to read it. Were the contents insulting or accusatory? He needed a moment, so he pulled out the parchment within and saw that it contained all of four or five lines. He scanned them. It was complimentary, if anything, so why was he being cast off?

"I truly am sorry," the dean said.

The man was sincere, but the matter was well and truly concluded. Hugh inclined his head and left.

Hugh's mirror image reflected sandy-blonde hair and hazel eyes. He stood a little over six feet tall and had fine enough facial features, but he was ordinary. He was a middle child of five, the third-born son. What were his prospects? What would he do now?

Failure, an inner voice accused.

He walked to a chair and sat, feeling like such a failure.

~~~

Nearly three weeks later, Hugh stepped into his father's study. "You rang?"

His father smirked and looked up at him. "What is that on your lip and chin? I've been meaning to ask."

Hugh lifted a brow as he stroked the hair growth on his chin. It had finally grown from stubbly to smooth. "And you call yourself an educated man."

His father laughed. By title, he was Lord Fitzwarren, although there was no estate to speak of. There hadn't been for generations. He had been a professor of religious studies and his students had called him Professor Fitz. "I think you should go join your friends."

Hugh cocked his head. "Uh—"

"You were planning on it before the position came along. Were you not? Go. It will do you good."

"They're not expecting me. I don't even know if the others are still there."

"You know Joel is there. And presumably his wife. The two of them were head over heels in love, last I heard."

"They are."

"So, go. What's the place called again?"

"Manoria."

"Manoria. That's right. Take the curricle. It's cold but you're young. The excursion will do you good. Go clear your head." He paused before sobering. "It's been long enough, son. What happened was not your fault."

Hugh took a moment to respond. "I never thought it was," he replied evenly. What he felt was regret, not guilt.

"It was a terrible thing that happened, and you got caught up in the consequences. You were not treated fairly."

Hugh wasn't certain if he agreed with that assessment or not. In any event, he was spared from replying because of the approach of his younger sister Selena. He turned to look at her.

"Someone is here to see you," she said warily. "The boy's mother," she whispered.

Hugh was stunned. "Offer her tea, will you?"

"I did. She declined. She seems … apologetic."

Apologetic? "I need to get something and then I'll be right in. Will you tell her?"

His twenty-two-year-old sister nodded and went to do it. Hugh looked at his father, who was clearly concerned, and then returned to his room for the letter.

Royden's mother, Lady Olanders, sat in their drawing room with her gloved hands folded in her lap. Dressed in unrelieved black, she looked pale and lost.

"Lady Olanders," Hugh said.

She wore a poignant expression. "Mr. Pritchett."

Hugh took a seat across from her. She had dark hair and strong features. He could see the resemblance to Royden, but the features had worked better on a male face. "I am terribly sorry for your loss."

"Thank you. I am sorry you lost your position. You were my son's favorite professor."

It took a few moments to respond. "That is a surprise to hear," he admitted. "I never got that feeling."

A pained smile crossed her face. "No, you wouldn't. That was his way. He liked keeping his cards close. He was always testing. Pushing the boundaries to see how far he could go."

Now *that* sounded like Royden.

"Because of you, I saw my son ... the day before."

Hugh nearly cringed. "I see. Well—"

"Oh, he knew he was deserving of being made to leave," she interjected. "That's why he respected you. So many wouldn't, you know. He called you spools."

"I beg your pardon?"

"Spools. As in spools of thread. He said that his teachers and professors were the spools wound with the threads of their knowledge."

"Ah."

"Some had substantial thread, others were weak and flimsy."

7

It was an odd comparison, but Hugh could understand it.

"But most spools, this is his observation, not mine, have become spongy and fat over time, their thread weakened. It doesn't matter. If the thread breaks, they simply unspool a length more. A student could grab hold and run with it, but that would never affect the spool. Not spools with tenure. They had long ago realized they only had to put up with students for a brief time before going back to their spongy spool lives."

It was not a complimentary observation, and yet Hugh knew those professors.

"Your core, however, is solid. He said he could pull your thread and you would yank back and then use it as a whip."

"Thread doesn't make much of a whip," he said with a wan smile.

She looked down at her hands. "I realize, of course, that I should have sent word and asked to see you rather than showing up unexpectedly." She looked up at him. "The truth is, I was afraid you might refuse. I have no one to talk to about him."

"I'm very glad to receive you, Lady Olanders. I wish I'd known him better."

"Thank you for saying so. I fear not many share that view, but he was a wonderful young man to me. To his sisters." She opened her reticule and pulled out a handkerchief, but it seemed more for something to do than because she needed it. "My husband is not an easy man. He believed he thought he was doing right by the boys, but he wouldn't listen to me. Boys need kindness and affection as much as girls. You do not make them stronger by berating and belittling them."

"You're right," he agreed. He hesitated before inquiring, "How are your other children managing?"

"As well as they can. It is difficult for the girls, as one would expect. Royden was my second born son and he and girls were close, especially after … his elder brother passed," she added with effort.

The words came as a jolt. "I'm sorry," Hugh said.

She studied him. "You didn't know, did you?"

"No."

"They know at the university. Everyone we know knows about it. And they all judge. They usually keep their distance from us if they can. The children have their friends, of course."

It must have been a scandal of some sort, then, because an accident or an illness would have provoked sympathy, not judgment.

"He hung himself," she said, peering unflinchingly at him.

"My God," he breathed.

"He was fourteen. A child. A thoughtful, loving child." Her gaze went vacant as she looked inward. "The boys were so different. Robert was an excellent student, a dreamer, slight of build, although he might have grown out of it. Royden was boisterous and restless, constantly getting into mischief. My husband preferred *that* over the demeanor of his brother." She paused. "I believe Robert possessed too sensitive a soul for this world. His death—"

Her voice faltered, and all he could think was, *two sons committing suicide*. How was it even borne?

"It was devastating for all of us, but I see now that it might have been the most damaging to Royden. The girls were younger, five and seven. Royden was eleven. Afterwards, his father became even harder on him. To his way of thinking, Robert had been too soft. Defective," she added with a curl of her lips. "Can you imagine a man saying that to his wife when she has lost her child?"

"No," Hugh replied quietly.

She looked down at the hanky she had been twisting. "I understand my son left a letter for you."

He pulled it from his pocket and offered it to her. "It's more of a note."

She looked at it and, for the first time, her eyes filled. "Will you read it to me? I forgot my glasses."

"Of course." He opened it and read.

> *Dear Professor,*
>
> *I wish I would have known you when I was younger, that you had served as my mentor. It would have done me good to know that character, strength and kindness <u>can</u> coexist in a man. My participation in the tomfoolery during class was cruel and disruptive, and I regret it. I hope you will forgive me.*
>
> *Sincerely,*
>
> *Roydon Cimmeron*

Lady Olanders sat perfectly still. "He said as much to me," she finally uttered. She swallowed and looked away. "I believe he had made up his mind to do what he did before he saw me. He came to say goodbye."

Hugh's breath caught.

"Not that he made it obvious," she continued as she met his gaze again. "But there was something, a comment he made. He said, out of the clear blue, that Robert was absolutely fine, frequently dining at the same table with Christ himself. Probably evaluating the wine. He said the church didn't know what the bloody hell they were talking about. Robby's soul was not damned."

He gave her a gentle smile, "I don't believe so, either." She sighed with what looked to be a release of tension and then put her handkerchief back into her reticule. She stood, and he stood with her.

"Meeting you has helped," she said. "Thank you, Professor Pritchett."

"I'm not a professor anymore, Lady Olanders."

She reached out as if to touch him, but then lowered her hand. "You will always be one to me. The best of them." He was touched to the point of feeling emotional. He gave her a tight smile and showed her to the door where he bid her goodbye. When he'd closed the door and turned around, he saw his father and sister waiting at the end of the hall. "I'm alright," he assured them.

"That poor woman," Selena uttered.

It was an understatement. The loss was incomprehensible. He nodded and started toward them. "I think you're right about me going to Manoria," he said to his father. He suddenly and desperately needed an escape.

"Good," the older man approved.

"I'll leave in the morning."

"In the meantime," Selena said. "Do you want to play a game of chess?"

Hugh gave her a look of amusement and affection. "You are terrible at chess."

She huffed. "Terrible is an exaggeration. Besides, I learn something every time we play. One day I'll win. And, oh, how I will crow about it."

He grinned. "How about a card game instead? Something you actually stand a chance of winning."

She smirked. "As a matter of fact, now I *will* win. Papa? Care to join us?"

"Why not?" the older man replied affectionately. As they started to the parlour, he threw his arm around Hugh's shoulders and squeezed. "I feel I've already won."

Hugh Pritchett

<u>Chapter Two</u>

Wednesday, December 12th

Charlotte Richards rode alongside her cousin, Virgil Knox, in his new, very fine carriage. He had recently received a sizable inheritance and was spending it lavishly. Not that it was any of her business. Virgil was thirty-six and well educated. He was accustomed to having money and spending freely. She hoped his funds would hold out because he would not know what to do if he had to economize.

The two of them were on a sojourn to visit family and friends. They'd just spent a few days with an elderly great aunt, Great Aunt Tessa, whom they'd always called Gatty, and were on their way to an estate called Manoria, the home of her friend, Jane, and Jane's husband Joel. So far, the journey had been enjoyable. Charlotte and Virgil had appreciated good meals, perused local shops and attractions, and stopped whenever they were tired. They'd stayed at quality inns where they had each been provided with lovely rooms, and Virgil had gladly paid for it all. The only thing that had been an irritant to Charlotte was that she would have occasionally liked to read, but Virgil claimed he could not read in a moving carriage, so, he chattered away, and she obliged.

It got wearing.

"I fear the old girl may not make it to see her birthday," Virgil ruminated, speaking of Gatty. "But she certainly is enjoying planning the bash."

"Which is worth a lot," Charlotte replied.

"Remember when we were young, and she played cricket with us?"

Charlotte smiled. Who could forget? Gatty was not only a character, she was a competitive one. She aimed to win, even if playing with her great nieces and nephews. Charlotte hoped to be as spry and fun loving when she was old.

"You know what would make her happy?" Virgil mused.

"Well, let's see," Charlotte played along. "There is planning any bash at all, especially one that will honor her. Eating sugared figs and then licking her fingers. Sipping scotch whiskey—"

"Seeing us engaged," he interrupted.

Charlotte's grin instantly vanished. What had put such a nonsensical notion in his head, she did not know, but she wished he would stop bringing the subject up. As she had established! Marrying him would be like marrying a brother if she'd had one. The idea of it was not only ludicrous, it was off putting. "You promised you would not bring the subject up again," she replied crossly.

"It was for her sake, this time," he said sheepishly.

"I'm sure she *would* like to see us each happily married, but *not* to one another. She would find the thought of it as absurd as I do." She folded her arms. "Do you want to ruin the trip for me?"

"Of course, I don't, but I don't see why it's so absurd."

She heaved a noisy sigh of annoyance and looked out the window.

"Oh, Charlie," he cajoled. "Give me two minutes to make my case. Just two minutes."

She looked at him with a scowl. "You know I loathe when you call me Charlie. It might be an adorable nickname for a lady who is delicate and petite and pretty as the day is long, but not for me. Not for one who stands five feet, ten inches tall and is as plain as milk."

"I like your height," he rejoined. "Tall people are taken more seriously. But, fine. I will not call you Charlie ever again. Now, may we return to the other topic?"

3

She bit on the tip of her tongue for a moment. "If I give you the two minutes you requested, will you promise not to bring up the matter again?"

He held up his hand in a pledge. "I will agree not to say one more word on this subject ... for the rest of the year."

The rest of the year was only a matter of a few weeks, but she was stuck with him on this trip. When they returned to the city, she could and probably would avoid him. Eventually, he would get the point. He had been a playmate throughout her life, and she loved him, but not in *that* way. She had been as clear as she could be on the matter. She could only hope and pray he would stop pestering her about it before she was forced to divulge that she found the idea repugnant. "Two minutes," she said coolly.

He took out his pocket watch and consulted it before meeting her gaze. "You and I are the best of friends. We enjoy one another's company, and we respect one another. None of that will change throughout the coming years."

This was so uncomfortable, but she'd given him the two minutes.

"We make a handsome couple, and we would have fine, strong children. We're distantly related enough that it wouldn't be strange. In fact, I think it would delight all the family. We run in the same circles, share similar views. In fact, the only aspect I can think of that you might initially object to is the thought of ... physical intimacy.

She cringed that he had said it. How excruciatingly awkward this was!

"As to that, it is merely a physical act," he added beseechingly. "To achieve a certain goal for the most part. Any initial, uh, embarrassment or awkwardness, while perfectly natural, would not be permanent. In fact, I would venture to say that the awkwardness is a normal consequence in any marriage." He paused, looking at her searchingly. "Your thoughts?"

"Have you made all your points?"

He hesitated. "Well enough, I think."

She shifted to face him fully. "Virgil, my affection for you is deep and abiding, but it is the fondness one feels for a member of one's family. I am not worldly, nor would I ever claim to be, but nor do I think I am naive. I very much hope to fall in love one day, but if I do not, I could be satisfied enough as a spinster. That would not be my preference, but I cannot see myself marrying without being in love. Romantic love."

He scoffed. "Romantic love does not last. It is a fleeting thing. Show me one middle-aged couple who are still in love."

"Even if that's true, which I don't believe it is, surely the romance mellows into something equally precious." She noticed that his expression was set. He wasn't even listening. "Oh, Virgil. Why would you ever consider settling for a wife without being in love? You have everything going for you and scores of eligible ladies to choose from."

"I don't want one of them. I want you."

Spoken like a five-year-old, she thought.

"I see it so very clearly in my mind," he wheedled. "How perfect we'd be. Can't you see that?"

"No," she replied quietly with a shake of her head. "I cannot. I could never see you that way."

He snorted. "I don't believe spinsterhood would be satisfactory. You're meant to be a wife and a mother. A lady with a fine house to run. That's the life that's meant for you."

She hoped so, but it would never be with him. "Each of us must discover our own path," she rejoined tenderly. "Following the dictates of our hearts and minds, we make the choices that make up our lives."

He harrumphed. "So, it is *you* who will ruin *my* trip."

"Don't be silly. And please don't pout."

He stuck out his bottom lip. "I'll pout if I want to."

It was good to see him tease. "Alright," she said lightly with a shrug. "Have it your way. I will be reading," she said reaching for her book.

"Reading is so boring," he objected.

"Reading is not boring. But, fine. Think of a game, then."

He thought about it. "The Minister's Cat. You start. Any letter you choose."

She grinned. That was more like it. "And kindly remember you have promised not to bring the subject up again."

"For the remainder of the year," he clarified before making a buttoning motion over his tightly closed lips.

She nearly rolled her eyes but, on second thought, she would take her victories where she could get them.

Charlotte Richards

Chapter Three

On Friday afternoon, the fourteenth of December, Hugh drove into the long, curved driveway of Manoria and abruptly reined in the horses with a gasp; the house was so stunningly grand! Of course, he knew certain facts such as the place had been built as a hunting lodge more than a century ago, and his friend, Joel, had inherited it along with a marquisate from a distant cousin. But criminy! Look at it!

Joel, along with his twin brother, Jonathan, and another close friend Dab, had first seen it last Christmas. When they returned home, Joel commented it was 'quite something' and larger than he and Jonathan had remembered. Hugh recalled one of them saying it was impressive, but he had certainly not been expecting *this*. It struck him as a gothic mansion. Its tall, three-story center fronted shorter wings that were set back at a slight diagonal.

He huffed an astonished laugh, but then sobered. The sight he beheld was just another example of how he felt separated from his friends. Not that they would leave him behind. They were all tried and true, loyal to the end, but every single one of them, Nigel, Joel, Jonathan, Dab and JG, had fallen in love in the last few years. Three of them had married their ladyloves, and the other two had plans to do so. Two had come into an unexpected inheritance and wealth. In Joel's case, it had also resulted in a rise in his station. He had then passed on the barony to his brother. Since JG was already heir to a dukedom and a fortune, Hugh was the odd man out.

He would never possess wealth. No unexpected inheritance would be coming his way. Nor was he in love, which was probably a good thing since he had nothing of substance to offer a lady. Still, observing his friends, he could not help but feel a twinge of envy at their happiness and newfound places in the world.

He drove on and parked. He climbed down, stiff from the drive and the chill, and stretched. The sky was filled with low-hung, gray clouds that warned of impending precipitation as Hugh walked to the front door and knocked.

It was opened by a smart looking butler of perhaps forty with silver hair. "Good afternoon, sir," the man greeted pleasantly.

"Good afternoon. I'm Hugh Pritchett."

"Welcome!" He stepped back. "I'm Reedman."

Hugh glanced back at the carriage as a spry, young man bounded toward it. The lad smiled at him and doffed his cap. Hugh waved a hand in response and then stepped inside. "The thing is," he said as he took off his hat. "I'm not exactly expected."

Reedman closed the door behind him. "A room stands ready for you at any time, sir."

The statement was heartening.

A footman stepped up to take Hugh's outerwear, which Hugh shrugged off and handed over.

"He'll be in the ivy room," Reedman said.

"Very good, sir." The footman walked on.

To think! This grand manor with servants was Joel's new world. It was mind boggling. Joel and Jonathan had come from the same sort of modest existence as he did.

The spacious entry hall was no less awe-inspiring than the exterior. Large paintings and tapestries and mounted heads of stag hung on the walls. A fire burned brightly in a massive stone hearth across the room. On either side of it were arched entryways, the center one was large and led to the dining hall, the other was smaller and dim. "I find myself overwhelmed," he admitted. "My friends failed to prepare me for the grandeur of this place."

Reedman murmured his understanding. "It frequently hits me still, and I've been here a dozen years. May I offer you a tour, Mr. Pritchett? Or would you prefer to be shown to your room or to the salon or drawing room for a drink?"

"I'd love a tour, if it's convenient."

"Perfectly convenient, sir."

"Are the others about?"

"Not the gentlemen. They went riding and they planned to go into the village. The ladies are in the west wing drawing room involved, I believe, in a quilting circle."

"Ah."

"I should think the men will be back soon," Reedman added.

"Knowing my friends, I imagine that depends on the quality of ale at the tavern."

"It's quite good," Reedman replied with a smile. He gestured and then started forward. "This original structure was built early in the last century. The wings of the home were added later."

Hugh recalled Joel saying as much.

"This floor contains the reception areas and dining room. Straight through, is an office, a library and more. That doorway leads to the upper floors. Your room is on the second floor."

"Up the haunted staircase?" Hugh teased, using the term Joel and Jonathan had given it as boys when they visited.

Reedman chuckled. "It's much less so now. Sconces have been installed, lovely things with mirrors. Do you know the work of Jeremy Alward?"

Jeremy. Alice and Jocelyn's cousin, who was a brilliant artist and yet slightly touched. "I do. I've had the good fortune of meeting him. His work is amazing."

"Oh, indeed," Reedman agreed.

He followed Reedman into the dining hall. The long table must have seated twenty. His family would have filled it out nicely, although there wasn't sufficient space in their home for it. "Is there a crowd in residence? I have no idea which of my friends is still here."

"I believe they all still are," Reedman replied. "You are the eleventh guest to arrive, but two since returned to the city. Miss Walston and her aunt, Lady Vinson."

"Oh. I'm sorry I missed them," he said sincerely. There were people who added life to a party. Lakely Walston, Nigel's sister, added fireworks. She rarely held back a comment or an opinion no matter how controversial it might be. Lady Vinson, on the other hand, they called her Monty, was elegance incarnate. She must have been nearing fifty, but she was still a beauty. She was that rare combination of sophisticated and yet humble. Since she had no children of her own, she was particularly close with her nephew and nieces. "The number of guests must be a strain on the staff," Hugh mused.

"No, not at all. There are normally ten of us, eight inhouse, but we increased the number for the party."

Ten staff members for a family of three. Well, a family of three and a large manor that reminded him of a gothic mansion.

"The kitchens are below," Reedman continued. "The east wing houses the staff and a schoolroom. The family chambers, a few guest rooms and a conservatory are in the west wing. Other guest rooms are upstairs, directly above us."

"Will a map be provided?" Hugh jested.

Reedman chuckled. "You won't need it." He paused before continuing. "Breakfast selections are set out in the morning, or we can bring a tray to your room, if you prefer. It's really quite informal. Food is set out and guests can enjoy luncheon whenever they wish. Tea is served at one, and aperitifs and hors d'oeuvres are offered at five. Dinner is served between six and seven."

Hugh studied the tapestries. They were Persian, probably seventeen-century. The reds, purple and gold were still vibrant. Each one would have taken an entire family more than a year to complete.

Beyond the dining hall was a corridor that led to a small library, a smoking room, a drawing room, an office, and a large, wood-paneled privy room. They had started back toward the dining hall when the housekeeper approached.

"This is Mrs. Wahl, the housekeeper," Reedman introduced. "Mrs. Wahl, this is Lord Stewart's good friend, Mr. Pritchett, who has just arrived."

She inclined her head. "Please let us know anything we can do to make your stay more comfortable."

"Thank you, Mrs. Wahl."

"More guests have arrived," she said to Reedman. "Miss Richards and a Mr. Knox. He was shown into the salon at his request, but she hoped she might join your tour."

"I've met her," Hugh said. "She is delightful company."

"I'm so pleased to hear it," a female voice said as Charlotte stepped into the corridor. "I lagged behind there for a moment, caught up looking at everything."

She wore a simple, pale gray traveling gown that suited her beautifully. Her warmth and enthusiasm were so genuine, it enveloped Hugh like a hug and gave him a lift. "Hello," he said. "It's nice to see you again."

"You as well," she returned.

"I'm Reedman, Miss Richards," the butler said with a bow of his head. "I hope your journey was pleasant?"

"It was, thank you, Reedman. I have no complaints at all."

Mrs. Wahl was making a silent retreat.

"I've just shown Mr. Pritchett this area of the home—" Reedman said.

"I wouldn't mind seeing it again," Hugh interjected.

Charlotte nodded. "It's amazing, isn't it?" she asked Hugh.

She had brown eyes. Lovely eyes. He hadn't remembered that. He'd remembered her wit and her height and how likeable she was, but not her eyes. "It is. I told Reedman my friends hadn't prepared me for the splendor."

"I'm not certain one can be prepared," she replied. "Jane told me about it in detail. I'm so nosy, I must have had a hundred questions. But seeing it is a wholly different experience."

"Then off we go," Reedman said cheerily. "And then I suggest we see the kitchens, the wine cellar, and then, perhaps, the family wing. That's where the ladies are gathered."

"Involved in a quilting circle," Hugh said to Charlotte.

"So I heard. For the expectant mother, I imagine," she replied with a twinkle in her eyes. "I cannot wait to see her."

He was so glad she'd joined them. She most definitely added life to a party. In fact, she'd just stirred up some life in him.

3rd Marquess & Marchioness of Larrowford

Joel Stewart and Jane Lloyd Stewart (nee Kingman)

Manoria of Glouchestershire

Chapter Four

Five ladies sat in a quilting circle in the west wing drawing room of Manoria. Among them were the mistress of the house, Jane, (Lady Larrowford) her younger sister, Alexandria Kingman, (Lady Alexandria) and Alice (Mrs. Alice Walston) who was well advanced in her first pregnancy. The quilt they worked on was for the baby.

Alice's sister, Jocelyn, (Miss Weatherly) sat next to her, and Theo, Dab's new wife, (Lady Sonden) rounded the group out. Each lady had a bag within reach containing squares of cloth for the quilt. Alice and Jocelyn's mother and sisters had sent many of them from their home in Boston.

Alice studied a square of blue silk. "I think this was from the gown that matched that doll," she said to her sister.

"Oh, yes," Jocelyn replied with a laugh. "Alice and I both were given gowns one year along with a matching one for our dolls."

Theo smiled. "We did that, too. I wish I still had that doll."

Jocelyn sighed. "I am so ready to be married."

Alexandria glanced up at her. It had seemed an out of the blue comment.

"It won't be long now," Jane consoled.

"I suppose not," Jocelyn agreed. "Although, in all honesty, it feels more like Lord Morguston's day than ours. It's his guest list for the most part."

Alexandria tried not to react, even though she didn't think that would be a bad thing, at all. It would be an event written about in the society columns. She wouldn't have complained about it. In fact, it should have been her lot.

Last season, which was supposed to have been *her* season, had been an abysmal failure she was still trying to live down. It's why she was sitting here sewing like an old lady with her sister's friends. The one and only reason she was visiting Manoria was to have a valid excuse not to attend the Christmas Cotillion. But it really should have been her marrying the heir to a dukedom and having a magnificent wedding filled with important and prestigious guests.

They would have described her in detail. Her loveliness. Her gown. Her radiance. Instead, it was Jocelyn. Simple, only merely pretty, American Jocelyn Weatherly. Of all the married or engaged ladies in the room, Jocelyn was the only one who would have a prominent wedding. It would be one of *the* weddings of the year.

Life made no sense.

Her own sister, Jane, the firstborn daughter of an earl, had thrown away her first season when she'd fallen in love with a soldier. A soldier! Who had then gone and died in the war, but only after they had married, and she was carrying his child. She'd ruined her life. Everyone said so.

After Hammond's death, Jane had closed herself off with her son, while society had marched on and forgotten all about her. Then came Alexandria's season and Jane decided to reemerge. Of all bloody times!

To Alexandria's way of thinking, fate had finally smiled on Jane when she met Joel Stewart. Initially, he had been a baron with no fortune, so no one Alexandria would have considered, but then he had inherited a marquisate and a rich estate. A catastrophic misunderstanding followed, but *no, no, no,* she would not revisit *that* humiliation.

In the end, Jane and Joel married in a small ceremony at the village chapel out of necessity after it became widely rumored that they had stolen away alone together. It was the truth, of course, leaked by Alexandria, although it was never supposed to have gotten so out of hand.

By all rights, Alice Weatherly ought to have visited London and left again for her home in Boston without taking the heart of a peer with her. Not that Nigel Walston was the prize Alexandria had set her sights on. He was only the son of a baron. Also, his father, Lord Merton, had a gambling fixation which might have, (could still, she supposed) annihilate the family estate. Still, Nigel and Alice had fallen in love.

After some rift nearly destroyed things between them, Nigel followed her to America, and they were married in a small church ceremony with only her family in attendance.

Theo was pretty. She was also quiet, shy perhaps, and private. Alexandria was not finding her easy to know. It was ironic that Theo, a penniless native of Dover, had caused the uproar she had by snaring the interest of Dabney Adams. London's Adonis. The papers hadn't been particularly kind in their description of her at first, but she'd won them over in the end. When she and Dab married, again in an intimate church ceremony, the papers gave a glowing account of her beauty.

Dab and his new bride, no matter who that bride had been, could have had *the* wedding of the year, not only because of his fame, but also he'd inherited his uncle's fortune. Instead, he had chosen to wed Theodora Martel and to live an obscure life.

Alexandria had no interest in leading an obscure life. Her plan, at the moment, was to stay removed from the social scene until she reentered with grace and great style in the spring. This time would be different. She would be clever and careful, chastened even, and *not* as choosy as before. Any handsome gentleman with an appropriate title and adequate means to keep her would do. She could make it happen. She *would* make it happen.

Alice shifted to stretch her back.

"How is the kicking?" Jane asked her.

Alice hesitated. "Not as much as it was. It only bothered me in one spot," Alice said as she touched the ribs on her left side. "Here."

"Arthur was like that, too," Jane replied. "As if he bore me a grudge."

Jocelyn chuckled and then leaned forward to talk to Alice's tummy bulge. "How many siblings would you like, darling? Would you like a sweet brother like Arthur?"

"The more important question," Jane spoke up, "Is how many siblings does Mamma want the baby to have?"

"It's difficult to know yet," Alice hedged.

"Off the top of your head," Jocelyn encouraged playfully.

Alice gave her sister a look. "How many children do you want?"

"Four," Jocelyn said boldly. "Perhaps even five."

Alexandria wrinkled her nose. "Really. I only want one or two. The obligatory son, of course. The heir. And, I suppose, a spare would be ideal."

"Well?" Jocelyn asked her sister.

"At least two," Alice said. "But may I have this one and then decide?"

Jocelyn looked pointedly at Jane. "We all have to answer now."

"I very much hope to have more," Jane replied. "I adore children and babies and motherhood. Joel will be such a wonderful father. He already is to Arthur." She looked at Theo. "What about you, Theo?"

"We want a large family," Theo replied shyly.

"Oh?" Jane asked with interest.

Theo nodded. "Dab would have loved having a sibling. I had four sisters. Even when we were arguing, I would never have chosen to be without them."

Alice smiled. "I can see you and Dab with a brood of little ones."

Alexandria couldn't quite picture Dabney Adams happily settled with his pretty little wife from Dover and a houseful of noisy children. It was too banal.

Jane peered at Alice. "Do you have a feeling if it's a boy or a girl?"

"No," Alice admitted. "Did you?"

Jane nodded. "Toward the end I did. I was positive it was a girl."

They all laughed. There was a knock on the door, and it opened to reveal Charlotte. "Hello," she cried.

Jane rose and set her sewing aside. "You're here!"

"I am. Is there room for one more in this merry band?"

"Of course," Alice and Jocelyn said in chorus.

Jane and Charlotte embraced.

"My gracious, Jane. This house is glorious!"

"Thank you. I am so glad you're here."

"So am I. What a wonderful place to celebrate Christmas."

"It is," Jane agreed. "Or rather it would be," she added with a nose wrinkle of regret. "But we are returning to the city this year. Arthur wants to see his grandparents, and they him."

"Of course, they do."

"You know everyone, I believe. Alice—"

"Yes," Charlotte said, looking at Alice. "You look wonderful, Alice. How are you feeling?"

"I'm well, now. The first months were not easy."

"That is an understatement," Jocelyn said. "Hello, Charlotte."

"Hello, Jocelyn. It's good to see you again."

"Have you met Theo?" Jane asked Charlotte.

"No," Charlotte replied.

"Theo," Jane said. "This is Charlotte Richards, one of my oldest and dearest friends. We were school chums together. Charlotte, this is Dab's wife."

Charlotte offered her hand to Theo who rose and took hold with a smile. "I know that much, of course," Charlotte said. "Anyone with eyes and access to a newspaper knows that. The mysterious Miss Theodora Martel who swept in out of nowhere and captured the heart of the enigmatic Dabney Adams. It's Lady Sonden now, is it not?"

"Not to our friends," Theo laughingly replied.

The pair of them, Theo and Charlotte, looked absurd, Alexandria mused. Theo was petite while Charlotte loomed above all of them. How dreadful to be so tall.

"And you know Alexandria," Jane said.

Alexandria smiled politely, as did Charlotte. Jane's chum had never liked her much if she wasn't mistaken. Not that it was worth losing sleep over.

"How are you, Alexandria?" Charlotte inquired.

"I'm well, thank you. I hope you are."

"Very well."

Jane pulled a chair up and Charlotte sat.

"Are you still traveling on to see your cousin?" Jane asked.

"Yes. After spending a splendid few days with you." Charlotte looked at Alice. "My cousin, Millie, is soon to give birth."

"Oh," Alice replied. "Her first?"

"Her second. The first is a three-year-old little boy that I haven't seen in nearly that long."

"Where is she?" Jocelyn asked.

"Bridgwater, one county over."

"You traveled with Virgil?" Jane asked.

"Yes. He's another cousin," Charlotte explained, directing it to Theo. "Millie's elder brother. He's like an annoying elder brother to me, too."

Alexandria had endured enough dull, female chitchat to last a lifetime, so she stood. "Will you excuse me? I fear I have a bit of a headache starting."

"Of course," Jane replied. "Feel better soon."

Alexandria made her escape, sighing luxuriously once she was outside the confines of the parlor.

~~~

"Has she changed much?" Charlotte asked Jane quietly when Alexandria was gone.

Jane considered. "I have thought yes, absolutely. And sometimes I think yes, somewhat. I believe she is trying to change. To be a better person."

"She's beautiful," Theo offered.

"Yes," Jane agreed. "She and my mother thought she would reign over last season, but Alexandria made a hash of it."

"Perhaps next season will be better," Jocelyn offered.

"One can but hope," Jane replied.

Charlotte picked up a few squares of fabric from the basket at her feet. "Hugh arrived just ahead of us."

Jane blinked in surprise. "He did?"

"Yes."

"I thought he couldn't make it," Alice said.

"So did I," Jane said. "He's been teaching at Cambridge," she explained to Charlotte.

"Well, he's here," she said. "He is so thoughtful and amusing. Reedman gave us a tour together."

"Hugh is wonderful," Jane agreed. "He has a great wealth of—"

Alexandria came back into the room. "Pardon me for interrupting. I left my shawl."

"I have some headache powder in the still room," Jane told her. "Ring and ask for it, if you think it will help."

"I shall. Thank you." She picked up her shawl and left, closing the door behind her.

"As I was saying," Jane continued. "Hugh has goodness and depth and a wealth of knowledge on so many subjects, but he is never condescending about it."

Charlotte could already tell that was true, although she looked forward to learning more.

~~~

Alexandria made her way back to her room with a light step. Hugh had great wealth, did he? She hadn't known, but she should not have been surprised. All of her brother-in-law's close friends had money and title.

Hugh seemed quieter than the rest and he'd gone primarily unnoticed by her. Not that she wouldn't prefer to marry a man of higher rank, but given how things had gone last season, it would make sense to have options. She'd need to learn more about Hugh Pritchett.

Chapter Five

Hugh was shown to the salon where Virgil Knox was stretched out with a glass in hand and the decanter of brandy in reaching distance. Apparently, the man was comfortable making himself at home. Virgil Knox had a pleasant face and a sturdy build. He was tall, probably six and a half feet tall. He wore quality attire including a tweed, cutaway coat.

The two of them chatted awhile, most of it centering around all things Virgil. His houses, carriages, business interests, friends of influence, and opinions. He asked intrusive questions about the value of Manoria and Joel's inheritance. Virgil had just received a lucrative one, himself, he said.

How nice.

For the most part, Hugh nodded, deflected, and dodged. He remained polite until he managed to extricate himself with the excuse of finding his room and 'seeing to something.' Virgil gave a cavalier wave that set Hugh's teeth on edge. Poor Charlotte, being stuck with such a pompous ass for the journey, although, perhaps, he was being too hasty in his assessment.

He got as far as the entry hall when his friends converged from the back of the home, laughing with surprise and delight to see him. They were windblown and red-faced from the exertion.

"You're here," Jonathan said, reaching him first and slapping his shoulder. "And there is something growing above your lip."

"I wanted to look more like Joel," Hugh returned.

"I can appreciate that," Joel said. "Welcome!"

"We thought you couldn't make it," Nigel said.

They were all talking at once.

"Is the term over?" JG asked.

"Let's hear all about it," Dab interjected. "Over drinks. I need a warmup. To the salon?"

"Um," Hugh resisted. "There's someone there."

"Who?" Joel asked curiously.

"Charlotte Richards arrived," Hugh explained.

"Oh! Good," Joel replied. "Jane was so hoping she'd make it."

"She did and she traveled with a cousin. A Mister Knox. Virgil Knox. He's not the worst sort, but—"

"Ah," JG said with a knowing nod.

"The trophy room it is," Joel said in a clandestine tone before leading the way. "Quietly, gents. With great stealth!"

Dab threw an arm around Hugh's shoulder as they all followed. "Do you have any problem drinking with the heads of decapitated beasts staring at you?"

Hugh laughed. "Well, it will be a first."

During the next hour, the six friends caught up with one another. JG was concerned with his grandfather's declining health, but he admitted, albeit guiltily, to having enjoyed the time away. It was easy to understand. JG's grandfather, Lord Morguston, was not the most pleasant of men in fine health. Add the irritation of feeling poorly and needing constant and intrusive assistance, and one almost shuddered to think.

Dab was happier than Hugh had ever seen him. His marriage to Theo, as well as the changes of the past several months had brought out the best in him. It was good to witness the transformation.

Nigel was eager for the new baby, but anxious about the birth. Understandably. Jonathan was impatient to marry Lakely, but the engagement would happen when she willed it. Joel, like Dab, was truly happy.

Hugh explained what had occurred with his position, although he glossed over the blow it had dealt him. "The truth is, I didn't flourish in the job," he concluded.

"I thought you would," JG commented thoughtfully.

"So did I," Hugh admitted. "But the joy of teaching is, well, teaching. Getting through to a person. Making a difference. Exciting them about learning something new." His friends were listening and nodding. "Were we such know-it-alls?" Hugh asked.

"You weren't," Joel replied. "And I don't think I was."

Everyone glanced at Jonathan.

"What?" Jonathan laughed. "Hardly ever!"

"Perhaps you simply had the wrong group of students," JG said.

Hugh shrugged. "I can tell you this much. I'm glad to be here amongst you all."

"We're glad to have you here," Joel said, lifting his glass. "You and your mustache," he added with a wink.

All the glasses went into the air.

"I may grow one myself," JG said. "What do you think? Would I be as debonair as this pair?"

"Oh, without question," Jonathan exclaimed. "Even moreso. But discuss it with Jocelyn, first."

"I'll tell you what I told the others," Dab said to Hugh. "Beware of this place. Of any wishes you make here. It is capable of *magic*."

Joel looked at Dab with a smile and a slow nod. "To think, only a year ago—"

It was as true as it was astonishing. A year ago, neither Joel nor Dab had yet married their respective ladies. In fact, Dab would not meet Theo until summer. Last Christmas had found him as he'd been for most of his adult life, harboring a dark secret, a grudge for his family, and a profound loneliness and sense of isolation despite his close friendships. Last Christmas, when he'd joined Joel and Jonathan here at Manoria, he'd made a wish to feel more. All three friends had made a wish and the wishes had subsequently come true. Perhaps, it was nothing but sheer luck. Or was there some sort of magic to the place? If there was, what would his wish be?

~~~

The dinner of herb-crusted veal chops, a variety of vegetables, and freshly baked bread was delicious, and Hugh had been famished. Candles glowed, wines were appreciated, and laughter abounded. Afterwards, they moved into the salon and enjoyed conversation and games.

Hugh, Jonathan and JG were the last to retired to their rooms. They were all on the second floor of the tower. The guest rooms were adequately spacious to accommodate a wide, four-poster bed, a wardrobe, dresser, a sitting area and a desk and chair.

Hugh's room was called the Ivy room because of the English ivy pattern on the wallpaper. It was the only busy looking thing in the room. The décor was minimal, the overall effect masculine but restful. The fire in the hearth provided sufficient warmth for the night, but the window casements rattled against a brisk wind. He wondered if it would keep him awake, but that was his last conscious thought before slumber claimed him.

<u>Chapter Six</u>

Hugh woke early. His friends were returning to the city in five days, some sooner, and he wanted to get as much packed into the time they had left. He would return with the last of them and be home for his families' Christmas dinner.

The corridor was quiet as he left his room. He went downstairs and stepped into the dining room a few moments behind Charlotte, who smiled to see him. It's likely she wasn't as pleased as he was.

"Good morning," she said.

"Good morning," he returned. "Did you sleep well?"

"Very."

As they breakfasted together, he learned more about her journey, an amusing, elderly great aunt, and the quilt for the baby. He told her about the ribbing he'd received regarding his mustache, although he needn't have bothered since it was still being joked about at dinner the night before.

"Well," she said. "I have seen you with and without it and can assure you it's merely a question of your personal taste and comfort. You look very agreeable both ways."

"Thank you." He sipped his tea. "Do you know what I was thinking would be exhilarating this morning? A horseback ride to see some of the property."

"I agree. May I join you?"

"I wish you would."

She smiled. "Then I shall."

The morning was bitingly cold, but bright and beautiful as they set out. The air smelled of pine and snow. They rode for an hour, warming with the exertion as they took in the scenery. The estate of seventeen hundred acres had tenants and farms, but they only saw one in the distance.

When they topped a crest, they stopped and dismounted to walk awhile. They could see for miles in all directions. In the distance, the River Severn sparkled like countless priceless diamonds each trying to outshine the others.

Hugh breathed deeply. All the space and beauty and the jollity of being with his friends had swept away the last cobwebs of his melancholy.

"It's magnificent," Charlotte exulted.

"Yes, it is," he agreed. Charlotte was so full of life. He suddenly wondered how it would feel to pull her close and kiss her. It was a fantasy of futility, and an uncharacteristic one at that, since he was a gentleman and she a lady.

"How blessed they are to have been gifted this," she said peering out at the water. She looked at him. "I've known Jane a long time and I have never seen her more happy and fulfilled. It's done my.heart good to be here and see it for myself."

"I feel the same. I met Joel, Jonathan and the rest of them when we were twelve."

"It's extraordinary that you've remained close throughout the years. Makes you wonder if Providence didn't have a hand in it."

He nodded. He had often thought so himself. "I will admit, I sometimes feel as though I'm—" he faltered. "I don't want to say I'm being left behind, as in an action on their part—"

She looked at him with curiosity. "I'm not following."

"It's just that my friends have done so well of late. None of us ever thought we have much in the way of wealth. I don't mean JG, of course. I meant the original five of us who attended Harrow."

She stopped and faced him fully, the reins held at her side.

"As boys, we didn't dwell on it, but in adulthood, one is forced to evaluate it."

She nodded. "Well, yes. Boys and girls, alike."

"But not exactly alike," he rejoined. "A man has the responsibility of finances. Of providing for his family. That consideration shapes everything."

She was listening intently.

"We are all the sons of barons, but Jonathan and I were in the same position in that neither of us would inherit the title because we have elder brothers. But that changed for Jonathan while I—"

She gave him a moment to finish the sentence. When he didn't, she said, "Jane mentioned you're teaching at Cambridge."

"I was." He paused. "I am no longer teaching at Cambridge."

"Why is that?"

He had been reticent to tell his friends the details of the matter, but there was something about Charlotte that invited trust. As they walked on, he found himself opening up and sharing one thing after another. His initial frustration with Royden Cimarron and his cronies, and the incident that led to expelling the young man from class. Learning of the suicide, his own forced resignation and his subsequent melancholy and feeling of failure. The visit with Lady Olanders. Charlotte never once interrupted. "It not only feels that I'm back at square one, but … three squares behind."

She frowned. "Because you didn't enjoy being a professor?"

"It's what I thought I wanted to do. It's what I've worked for. I always loved academics and arcane subjects like history."

She canted her head. "There's so much I want to argue with there," she stated. "Starting with … history is not arcane. It lives on because of its influence on who and what we become."

He admired her no-nonsense manner. She would never be one to feel sorry for herself for long or allow a friend to sink into self-pity if she could help it. Had he been wallowing in it? "Well said. What else?"

"It is not unusual for us, any of us, to start down a path believing it's what we want and that over there is our destination," she said with a wave of her gloved hand. "But on the way, things can change. Things do change. Things we couldn't have anticipated. A path forks or it simply ends in a tangle of brambles. To begin down a new path does not make one a failure."

He nodded slowly. "I did expect to walk a certain path and end up at a certain destination, and that path has indeed ended in brambles. So now I will backtrack and hopefully find a new path. I don't see it yet, and I wish I did."

"You will."

He smiled. "Do you know, I think it's easier to see things clearly on a day like this."

"It also helps to air things out," she said. "Don't hold it inside. Say it or shout it but have out with it."

"It does help. Thank you."

She grinned. "You're welcome. Listening and lecturing are two of my favorite things to do."

He chuckled. "Shall we start back?"

They returned their horses to a cheerful hostler and started for the house, but she hesitated. "Would it be alright to look in the carriage house, do you think?"

"I don't see why not. I'm interested myself." They strolled toward the two-story stone structure. "The finest carriages are in there. Mine is over there," he said with a wry smile, pointing to an open-sided shelter. The wagon and carriage that had come with the estate were parked next to his curricle.

One of the large doors to the carriage house stood open. They entered and took a moment to allow their eyes to adjust. The place had a pleasant smell of wood and leather. At least, he found it pleasant. Looking around, he saw it had four bays and a spacious tack room. Four impressive carriages were parked, but Hugh only recognized one of them, Lord Morguston's town coach. JG had brought the best.

They heard quick footsteps coming down a back staircase and turned to see a good-looking man in his mid-twenties with red hair.

"'lo," the man greeted with a ready smile.

"Hello," Hugh returned. "We were just taking a peek."

"They're something, are they not?" The man replied in an Irish accent. "I drove that one," he pointed at a blue landau. "For Lord and Lady Sonden."

"Ah," Hugh said. "He mentioned it. It's a beauty."

"It is, that. She was a dream to handle."

"We came in that one," Charlotte said gesturing to a fashionable black carriage with yellow wheels. "It belongs to my cousin."

"Aye, the chaise. Your driver said it was a fine ride. I'm MacShane, by the by. Brendan Alexander MacShane. My friends call me Zander. My employers generally call me MacShane if they call me anything at all. Lord and Lady Sonden being the exception. They're good people. Down to earth, as it were."

"Yes, they are," Hugh agreed. "I'm Hugh Pritchett, and this is Miss Richards."

"How do you do," Zander said with a tip of his head. "What a place this is, eh? Never seen the like, meself. Some of the others went into the village to stay, but not me. There's lodging upstairs, good food, plenty to do. Fact, if you'll excuse me, I'll be getting on to help Reg with the horses if I can." He put on his hat and doffed it. "Pleased to make your acquaintance."

"You, as well," Charlotte returned.

He left with a brisk step.

"Who does this one belong to?" Charlotte asked, stepping closer to the coach.

"JG's grandfather, Lord Morguston."

"Ah."

"Sadly, he is unwell. JG has enjoyed the time away, but he's feeling anxious to return and check on him.

Charlotte murmured her understanding.

He glanced around at the neat, wide-open place before looking back at her. "Are you ready for some tea?"

"Tea sounds wonderful."

The two of them left the carriage house and started for the house. "Thank you," he said when they'd nearly reached it.

"For what?"

"Listening. I feel unburdened, having shared everything."

There was a beat of silence before she replied. "I'm glad. I am always happy to listen."

He had a strong desire to kiss her cheek. Instead, he opened the door for her.

~

Hugh had just given her an intense and yet undecipherable look that made Charlotte's heart race. He opened the door for her, and she stepped through cautioning herself that she was being silly. She was a person others could, and often did, confide in. She was a good listener and a nice person, but desirable gentlemen did not attach romantic notions to her. She was not a lady men fell in love with.

They heard the voices of the others from the dining hall. It sounded as though everyone was up and about, and the aroma of savory foods and sweet, freshly baked goods accented the air. A hot cup of tea and a scone with clotted cream sounded delicious. And a correction of her perceptions was certainly in order.

Chapter Seven

The ladies continued their quilting that afternoon. Alice, Nigel, JG and Jocelyn were leaving the following day, so they wanted to complete as much as possible. The men bundled up and spent the day hunting. For Hugh, it was a bracing day full of camaraderie. He felt wholly alive.

It wasn't until evening that they everyone gathered again in the salon. Hugh wanted to converse with Charlotte, but, inexplicably, Alexandria seemed to have attached herself to him. Even given her notoriously poor performance in the marriage mart last season, there was no reason for her interest in him. She was a beauty and the daughter of an earl. Was it simply practice at flirting because he was one of the few unattached males available? Meanwhile, Virgil dominated Charlotte's attention.

Aperitifs led to a delectable dinner. The pheasants they'd bagged had been baked with mushrooms, and the rabbits, also caught that day, had been perfected by a wine and garlic sauce. Afterwards, the company made their way to the great room.

Theo and Jocelyn relaxed in front of the hearth conversing.

Joel and Jonathan continued an intense game of chess begun earlier in the day.

Charlotte, Jane, JG, Nigel and Alice played a lighthearted game of My Ship's Sailed, the object being to collect seven cards of one suit, and Hugh, Dab, and Virgil Knox sat to play pinocle. Alexandria quickly joined them.

Jonathan cursed at a move his brother made. They were twins, they were close, but they were fierce competitors.

The group of five laughed at JG's reaction to *almost* winning a hand. Hugh glanced over, grinning at his friend.

Dab dealt.

As they arranged the cards in their hands, Virgil said, "If I count correctly, there are three married couples in attendance, and two that are engaged to be married, although Miss Walston is not with us, at present."

Dab smirked. "I would say Jonathan and Lakely are more … engaged to be engaged."

Hugh chuckled. "I miss her company."

Dab grunted and nodded. "Lakely is a force to be reckoned with."

"That makes two of us then," Virgil said as he studied his cards.

The others looked at him.

"Engaged to be engaged, I mean," Virgil said. "Not necessarily a force to be reckoned with." He laughed at his own joke.

"Congratulations," Dab said. "To whom are you engaged? Anyone we know?"

Virgil looked confused and then pointedly glanced at Charlotte.

Hugh's amused expression vanished. He felt as though he'd been punched in the gut. "Charlotte?"

Virgil grimaced. "*Uhh.* Let's forget I said anything."

Hugh swallowed.

"It's not official," Virgil added.

"I had no idea," Dab said.

"She's very private," Virgil murmured. "Doesn't like people knowing her business."

"That leaves only a few of us who are unattached," Alexandria said brightly. Her blue-eyed gaze connected with Hugh's before she blushed and looked back at her cards.

How did she do that, Hugh wondered. Make herself blush. He couldn't stop himself from looking over at the table of five involved in their game. Charlotte was animated, having a wonderful time. He wished he'd chosen that group to join, but to what end? She was engaged? Or engaged to be engaged? Had there not been an opportunity for her to mention it? Or perhaps she hadn't seen the need. Simply because he'd felt an attraction to her, didn't make it reciprocal. But Virgil Knox? Really? The man was too puffed up and insipid for her.

On second thought, apparently not.

At quarter past eleven, Alice retired to her room, Jane went to speak to the cook, and most the others began a game called Rhymes. The first person began the game by addressing the person to their left and asking a question. The reply, a statement, had to be prompt and had to rhyme with the question before they then asked the person to their left a question. If one could not form a rhyming answer, the player was out.

Virgil claimed he'd had too much to drink to be sharp enough to win, so he stretched out on one of the settees and watched.

JG won the first round and began the second. He turned to Jocelyn. "Care you, my love, for a dance?"

She shrugged. "I confess there is a chance." She looked to Charlotte next to her. "I heard you purchased a dress of … yellow."

Charlotte nodded. "I did. I purchased it from that fellow." She looked at Nigel to her left. "Is your wife feeling alright?"

"I do hope so but she's out of my sight." To Jonathan, Nigel asked, "Is it true you have a pet parrot?"

"There he is, eating a carrot." To Alexandria, Jonathan asked, "Do you wear a nightcap when you sleep?"

She hesitated a moment. "I would rather take a leap." She giggled and turned to Hugh. "Do you enjoy teaching, sir?"

"It's been so long, it seems a blur." Hugh turned to Theo. "How do you find married life?"

She smiled. "I like my husband and he likes his wife." She playfully leaned into Dab. "Is that true or am I making that up?"

"My love for you overfillith my cup," he replied to a tickle of amusement. He looked at Joel. "Are you going abroad or is that a rumor?"

"It's either that or I have a sense of humor." Joel looked to JG as the game had gone full circle. "Is a rhinoceros larger than a hippo?"

JG drew breath, but he was stumped. "Oh, I see how you are," he complained amidst jocularity at the round's first casualty. "Next time we'll reverse directions. You just wait."

Joel smirked. "Jocelyn, do you have a mink stole?"

"That's not mink, it's from a mole." She looked at Charlotte. "Do you think you are kind, or are you cruel?"

"Oh, nice! To the point of being a fool."

"We need a metronome," JG commented. "And it should move faster and faster. In the meantime, I'll tap my foot."

Charlotte asked Jonathan, "Did we meet at the ballet once?"

He shook his head. "It was a play in Paris, Fruntz." His mispronunciation was met with jeering. "Alright. Fine," he conceded. "I'm out."

Charlotte asked Alexandria, "Where do you have your gowns made?"

"From my maid," Alexandria replied, which drew a laughing thumbs down reaction. "What? It should count," she complained. "Made is different than maid."

"Not the sound of it," Jane said as she reentered the room. "You are out, and I'll take your place. Budge over." She sat and looked at Hugh. "Do you know you're one of my favorite people?"

"Would you swear it in a church with a big, tall steeple?"

JG's foot picked up speed and Jonathan joined in.

"What in the world do you see in Dabney?" Hugh asked Theo. She drew breath but couldn't reply fast enough and JG made a rude sound. "When did you begin wearing spectacles?" Hugh asked Dab.

Dab was stumped. He wagged a finger at Hugh. "Like JG said, turnabout is fair play."

The game went on until it was down to Joel and Charlotte. Jocelyn had been stymied by the word nature, Nigel with the word handsome, Jane with the word thousands, and Hugh with the word Venus. The only obvious reply he could think of was not a word he would utter in mixed company. Joel finally won amid great amusement.

~~~

The fire in the hearth illuminated the room dancingly, creating mysterious shadows as Alice lay in bed propped against a mound of pillows, her hands resting on her abdomen. Was the unborn babe within her in a state of sleep? She'd felt so little movement the last several days, it was worrying. Perhaps she should never have ventured so far from home.

The time they'd spent at their family's country home, Merton Park, had been relaxing and enjoyable. The fresh air and the cooler temperatures had revived her after the bottomless fatigue and sickness she'd suffered in the first months of pregnancy.

Her fingers drifted to the spot that had felt pummeled from within. It wasn't that long ago that she'd wished the kicking would stop – and now it had. It was her secret fear. What if something was wrong with the baby, and it was punishment for her traitorous thought? Tears filled her eyes.

"Move all you need to," she murmured. "Kick if you want. I won't complain again. I swear it. I wish I could kick myself." Could the baby somehow know her feelings? "Please be alright."

Please, please. Be alright.

Mrs. Alice Walston (nee Weatherly)

'Alice ... (had) fair hair, delicate bone structure and eyes of two different colors, one blue and one green, a curious birth defect of some sort. She was clever, but her mother feared she had more imagination than good sense. She fancied herself a writer, and was forever scribbling down stories, weaving tales and delving into research.'

Chapter Eight

As the party wound down and people began making their way to their rooms for the night, Virgil and Charlotte stood conversing quietly. What was the subject of discussion, Hugh wondered. He made his way to his room feeling disheartened.

Virgil Knox? *Really?*

In his room, he whipped off his cravat as he began to pace, alternately loosening and pulling the fabric taunt to achieve a satisfying pop. Virgil was glib and loquacious, but if his boasting was based on truth, he was wealthy. He was also tall and good looking enough. He wasn't unkind or unintelligent. And he was wealthy. Whoever became Mrs. Virgil Knox would not lack for any material possession.

He stopped, sighed, and tossed his cravat on the dresser thinking of a chant Lakely had come up with as a girl. *'Hugh is the mild one, Jonathan's the wild one, Joel is more well behaved. Nigel is our brother, so why would we bother? Dab has an oh-so-handsome face.'* She'd said it dozens of times to annoy them. She and Ada had skipped rope to it. It hadn't really bothered Hugh. All told, it wasn't a half bad assessment. It hadn't bothered him … until now, which was patently absurd.

He walked over to the mirror above the dresser and tilted it to look at himself. "Face facts," he murmured. Could he have done better in the classroom? Probably. Could he have tried harder to reach the more difficult students? Yes. He could have attempted to meet with them individually to get to know them better and to come to a meeting of the minds.

That said, he had tried. He had cared, prepared well, and he had tried. He was sorry about Royden. He would always be sorry. He was sorry for Lady Olanders and her daughters. Even for Lord

Olanders, whom he'd never met. What a horrific thing to lose two sons as they had.

Charlotte had been right. What happened had resulted in a new path for him. A new path, not the end of the world. There would be no more feeling sorry for himself. He would never possess wealth, but his wife, if and when there was one, would not be someone who required it either.

He stepped back. He was nowhere close to being ready for sleep. He started for the door but came to a halt. He closed his eyes and thought of Royden. "I hope you are dining with your brother," he said quietly. "Having fine wine and reflecting on the joys you knew." He opened his eyes, and nodded, feeling better for having said goodbye, as silly as that might be.

He left his room. It was silent in the corridor. He went back to the salon, but no one remained. There was really only one person he'd been hoping for, but his dictate about feeling sorry for himself would hold. "Tomorrow is another day," he said softly.

He retraced his steps, went through the dining room and headed for the library for something to read, but a glance into the parlour stopped him short. Charlotte was there and she sat alone. She was on the settee facing the fire in the hearth. His heart gave a lurch. "Hello," he said.

She looked over her shoulder and smiled. "Hello."

"May I join you?"

"Please do. I was having a final glass of brandy."

"That sounds good." He went and poured himself a glass.

"Tonight was fun," she commented.

"It was." He sat cattycorner from her. "I had a long ride to get here, but it was worth it from the moment I arrived. I draw strength from my friends."

She nodded. "I think we all do. Or most of us. Strength and perspective."

"Yes."

"I find myself curious about your family," she mused. "Will you tell me about them?"

"With pleasure. Well, let's see. My father, a very interesting man, studied classical studies before gravitating toward theology. He's a free-thinking former Methodist minister with a fascination for anything ancient Egypt."

She laughed. "How delightful."

"He was a bit too free-thinking for the church, so he ended up teaching at a small college of theology. He only retired from it a few years ago."

"Is he enjoying his retirement?"

"I think so. He keeps busy with research and he fills in at the college when he's asked."

"I am picturing an older you. Someone kind and good-natured and easy to talk to."

He smiled, rather liking the assessment.

"Are you close to him?"

"Very. I didn't fully realize it, but I based my concept of teaching on his experience. The difference was that his students wanted to learn. Wanted to listen and embrace all the knowledge they could acquire. When you have a student like that, there's nothing better in this world than teaching."

She nodded.

"I had a few of those," he continued. "But it's hard to give them the attention they deserve when you're dealing with the antics of showmen. The over privileged and under challenged. But I was thinking earlier that I could have and should have tried harder to reach them. My father used to say that the best teachers learn as much from their students as the other way around." He paused. "Some of my lessons have been learned after the fact."

"I believe the worst thing any parent can do is to give a child everything they wish for and to never make them responsible for any wrongdoing. Those children grow up expecting that to always be the case. We've all known and suffered those individuals. They're not exclusively young men."

"Agreed."

"What about your mother?"

"I always thought she was the typical loving mother most everyone had. Of course, there is no such thing. She's not perfect, but … I couldn't list three faults of hers."

"Really! I adore my mother, but I could list a dozen of her faults and not name them all."

He laughed. "Is that so? Name three."

"She is impatient. She does not suffer fools graciously, and … she laughs entirely too loudly for polite society."

"Whom do you take after?"

"They must both share the blame. I was raised to be curious, honest and forthright. I had no idea that wasn't the way of a proper young lady until I went to school."

"It ought to be the way of every young person."

"Yes. It should. Perhaps one day, many years from now, it will be."

"Was it lonely being an only child?"

She considered before replying. "I had my parents," she replied. "I also had cousins and neighbors for playmates. No, it wasn't lonely. I also went off to school when I was eleven. Miss Nevin's private seminary for young ladies. That's where I met Jane."

"And the two of you were fast friends, I imagine."

"We were."

"Being an only child is difficult to conceive when you come from a family with five children."

"I would have loved having siblings," she replied wistfully. "Without a doubt. And I would choose to have children, plural, for giving the gift of providing a sibling or siblings."

He blinked at the realization that *he wanted to marry her.* After the initial jolt of the thought, the insight felt like warm waves of assurance washing over him. "Your cousin, Virgil—"

She canted her head, waiting for him to continue.

"Is he a first cousin?"

"A second cousin, I think. They lived nearby, so we were frequently together. Millie, his younger sister was my close confidant for years."

"Where is she now?"

"She's in Bridgwater with her husband's family. She's in her confinement with her second child. Her parents-in-law are very doting. Virgil and I are going there for a visit when we leave here the day after tomorrow."

Damn. Too soon. He took a drink and looked into the fire."

"Now, you said you're the middle child, and you also said you had an elder brother."

"I have two elder brothers and two younger sisters. Only my younger sister, Selena, and I are still at home. The others are married and have families."

"Tell me about them," she urged. "And the Pritchett home. I want to feel as if I could walk in and know the place, as well as the family who's gathered for a family meal."

Her sincerity was obvious, but was she only after light conversation to while away the time? "I will gladly elucidate as long as you'll do the same."

"I'll be happy to but, as an only child, it will be a shorter and probably less colorful explanation."

He drew breath to speak but was distracted when Alexandria stopped in the doorway dressed in her nightclothes with a robe and shawl around her. Her hair was worn loose. She was a remarkably beautiful woman. He didn't particularly enjoy her company so he didn't always pay attention to it.

"Hello," Alexandria said. "I thought I might not find anyone up."

"Only the two of us," Charlotte said. "Chatting about our families. Join us."

Alexandria came closer. She sat next to Charlotte on the settee and looked at Hugh. "I would love to hear about your families."

"Would you care for a glass of brandy or port?" Hugh offered.

"No, thank you. I wouldn't mind a glass of warmed milk, though. Do you think it's too late to summon someone to fetch it?"

It was past one in the morning and Hugh had no doubt the staff was fast asleep. If not, they ought to be.

"I do," Charlotte replied apologetically.

There was a beat of silence before, "You're right, of course," Alexandria agreed.

Without question, Alexandria Kingman was used to being waited on. She probably never gave two thoughts to the staff. But perhaps he wasn't being fair. He didn't really know her. She was so extraordinarily different than Jane who was witty, amusing and all thoughtfulness. "It's amazing how different siblings can be," he commented.

Charlotte nodded. "You were about to tell me." She looked at Alexandria. "He is the middle child between two brothers and two sisters."

Alexandria's expression sharpened. "Are your brothers older or younger?"

"Older."

She seemed taken aback. "Ah."

A strange silence fell on them like a pall and then Alexandria fidgeted. A third person had changed the intimate dynamic of the earlier conversation. "It's not the most interesting topic, I admit," he said lightly.

"I find it quite interesting," Charlotte disagreed.

Alexandria looked at Charlotte. "Do you think cook would mind if I fixed myself a cup of warm milk?"

"Not at all. I can go with you if you like."

"That's so kind. You really are so kind."

"It's nothing," Charlotte said. She gave Hugh a regretful half-smile. "I hope we'll continue our discussion another time?"

"I look forward to it." The ladies rose, so he did the same. He bowed his head. "I wish you both a good sleep."

"Goodnight," Alexandria said in a somewhat cooler tone than she'd used with him before.

As the ladies left, he turned back to the fire with a shake of his head. Having two elder brothers seemed to have changed Alexandria's interest level. Ah, well. There would be no more flirting from her, but he'd found it disconcerting anyway.

Chapter Nine

Hugh's goal the next day was to spend time with Charlotte. It didn't matter if they rode or walked or played a game, he wanted her company and to get to know more about her. When he came down for breakfast, determined to seize the bull by the horns, plans had been made and were in motion all around him.

Alice and Jocelyn were upstairs readying themselves to leave.

Nigel and JG were all set to go.

Jane, Charlotte, and Theo had plans to go into the village, peruse the shops and have luncheon.

Joel was attending to business with his steward, a man named Triston Kerr, so Jonathan had arranged the morning's amusement for the rest of the men, an archery competition.

Hugh managed to share a smile and a nod of greeting with Charlotte, but no more. Hopefully, he'd have better luck in the afternoon.

~~~

An hour later, the ladies left for the village. Nigel, JG, and Jocelyn loitered around the carriage, waiting on Alice to join them.

In her room, cognizant of keeping them waiting, Alice stepped away from the chamber pot after relieving herself one last time. Her bladder was so weak these days. She lowered her skirts, glanced into the porcelain pot as she began to step away, and froze. There was *blood* in the pot. A slowly dissipating blot of blood.

Why would there be blood?

43

Filled with anxiety, she went to the bell and tugged it. It was soon answered by the housekeeper, Mrs. Wahl, who urged her to sit while she fetched her husband, sister, and tea – and off she went. Alice clutched her hands together, realizing only then that they'd gone cold. Her eyes filled.

Oh, God, she prayed. *Protect my baby.*

~~~

Hugh's arrow sailed over the target to an uproar of laughter and teasing. Archery was not his sport. He went to get the arrow. There was little chance of being wounded since everyone else could actually hit the target. Before he reached it, he noticed that JG's carriage was still there. So was JG, looking worried as he started toward the house. "JG," Hugh called. "I thought you'd left already," he called on the way.

"It's Alice," JG said when Hugh reached him. "We were waiting for her when the housekeeper came out. She summoned Nigel and then conferred with Jocelyn who sent me a panicked look before she rushed inside. I don't know what's happening, but something is amiss."

Hugh glanced at the house. "I wonder if there's anything we can do to help."

"Let's find out." JG replied and he led the way inside.

~~~

Nigel and Jocelyn were in front of Alice who sat stiffly in a wingback chair. Nigel was kneeling, Jocelyn standing with her arms crossed tightly. She had discreetly checked the pot. The contents were indeed pink and there looked to be a small dark brown clot on the bottom.

"We will send for the doctor," Nigel said evenly. "Just to be safe. There's probably nothing to worry about."

Alice nodded tightly. She had checked and she was not bleeding now. Nigel rose and kissed her cheek before leaving the room.

"It's too soon," Alice agonized, looking at Jocelyn.

"You must breathe and think calm thoughts. Remember what Papa always says. There will be plenty of time to worry once you know there's truly something to worry about."

"I wish he was here to say it to my face. I wish Mama was here. And Clara and even Sophia. I can't help thinking about her going into labor early. She could have died, Jaus. She could have lost the baby."

"But she did not, did she? She is fine and little Eliza is fine. I wish they were all here too, but it won't be so very long before they'll be here for the wedding and they'll be able to see their new little grandchild, whoever he or she may be," she added with an encouraging smile.

She squatted and grabbed hold of her sister's hands. "Ali, there's so much going on in there," she said with a look at her sister's swollen middle. "That," she said with a jerk of her head toward the chamber pot. "Is probably nothing at all. Do you have any pain?"

Alice shook her head. "No."

"Well, there you have it. You know very well that when the baby comes there will be pain."

There was a knock on the door and the housekeeper entered with a tea tray. Mrs. Wahl was a nice lady. She was quiet, but always ready with a kind word when needed. "How old are your children, Mrs. Wahl?" Jocelyn asked as she rose to her feet.

"Nine and nearly six." Mrs. Wahl set the tray on the table. "Noemi just turned nine. My son is Gabriel."

"A boy and a girl," Jocelyn said. "What are they like?"

"Noemi is the bolder of the two. She's often too bold to my way of thinking."

"Then Gabriel and Arthur are close to the same age."

"Yes. They are all three fast friends."

"That's wonderful."

"Is there anything I can get you?" The housekeeper asked, her gaze going from one to the other.

Jocelyn glanced at Alice, who shook her head, and then looked back to Mrs. Wahl. "I think we're fine. I believe the doctor is being sent for."

"Yes. It's being done. Just ring if you need anything at all."

"We will. Thank you." Mrs. Wahl left, and Jocelyn fixed Alice's tea and handed it to her. She had hoped Mrs. Wahl might prove a bit more engaging, but maybe there was no distracting Alice. "Here. Sip and breathe easily and think good thoughts."

"We mustn't hold up JG," Alice said worriedly. "I know how worried he is about his grandfather."

Jocelyn fixed her with a look. "Are you looking for things to worry about? Good gracious, every person here is quite capable of taking care of themselves. You have two to take care of, so sip your tea and think cheerful thoughts ... about how little sleep you are going to get once the baby is here. Remember how Sophia complained about Lola?"

"Sophia enjoys complaining."

"Yes, but Clara complained too," Jocelyn reminded her. "And she is not a complainer, generally speaking."

Alice leaned back, relaxing a little. "She didn't complain about Samuel that I recall. He has always been a dream child."

"He is," Jocelyn agreed. "But Stephen insisted on sleeping all day and wailing all night. Remember? Oh, just think of it. They'll be so changed when we see them again. Little people."

"I thank God you're here," Alice blurted. Tears spilled down her cheeks, which she wiped away.

"I know," Jocelyn returned tenderly. "I feel the same." She sat beside Alice. "It will be alright, Ali. I feel it. I truly feel that everything will be alright."

Chapter Ten

"Who shall set the pace today?" Astrid asked as she stepped outside and closed the door behind her. Miss Astrid Cayley was Mrs. Wahl's younger sister. She had a slender build and fair skin, like her sister. Their features were, in fact, quite similar, but Emilia Wahl had dark brown hair with an auburn cast while Astrid's was a pure, deep auburn.

She had come to Manoria with her sister with the intention of becoming a sort of governess to her niece and nephew. In other words, keeping the children from bothering anyone else. That's not how it had turned out. Not only had they been welcomed, they'd been made to feel wanted and valued. A tutor would be sought at some point in time but, for now, Astrid taught Noemi, Gabriel, and young master Arthur.

"It's cold," Gabriel complained.

"So, let's walk," Astrid said. "Chop, chop," she said clapping her gloved hands together.

"We don't want to walk today," Arthur announced.

"It's too cold," Gabriel said.

Astrid lifted a brow. "Which is why you have on your coats and shoes and gloves and hats and scarves. It's why I did not suggest us taking a walk in our birthday suits."

The familiar refrain made the children laugh. "I'll lead," Noemi said as she set out.

"One brisk circuit and then to the greenhouse," Astrid said, gesturing the boys onward.

They rolled their eyes but followed Noemi.

Astrid believed in taking fresh air every day and in physical exertion. The vast openness of the outdoors put one's struggles into perspective. She'd told the children as much, but it was something everyone had to discover for themselves. Problems loomed larger and weighed more when confined indoors, especially in small spaces.

"Hello," a man called.

She turned to see a stranger hurrying toward them, taking wide steps. A handsome stranger with red hair jutting below his cap. She drew in a sharp breath of cold air that she felt in her throat.

"Who's that?" Arthur asked.

"Good mornin'" the man greeted when he reached them. "Might I walk with you?" There was a moment of silence before he pressed a hand to his chest and ducked his head. "Beggin' your pardon. I should have introduced meself. Brendon Alexander MacShane, at your service." He bowed. "My friends call me Zander, and I'd be honored if you'd do the same."

He had red hair, brown eyes and a complexion that spoke of working outdoors. His wool coat was worn but respectable enough. His Irish accent was more pronounced than her mother's had been, but the familiar cadence stirred something in Astrid's chest.

"Are you one of the drivers?" Arthur asked.

"I am. I drove Lord and Lady Sonden from the city. Are you a driver?"

The children laughed.

"No," Arthur exclaimed. "We live here."

"Oh! Well, it's a fine place you have." He looked at Astrid. "Reggie has just informed me that you are Miss Cayley."

He was entirely too bold and forthright to her way of thinking. "I am."

"She's my aunt," Gabriel said.

"That would make you Sir Gabriel, and you must be Sir Arthur, and you are Lady Noemi. Amn't I right?"

Noemi lifted her chin, delighted to play along. "You are. We are walking one circuit, briskly, and then going on to the greenhouse to work on our projects."

"And may I join you?" he asked her.

"If Aunt Astrid says so."

Astrid was blushing hotly despite the cold, and anxious to get in motion before one of the children remarked on it. "Join if you wish," she said curtly. "Let's go" she directed to the children.

Noemi marched on, and the boys followed after glancing back at Zander with something akin to admiration. Astrid followed, and Zander fell in step with her. He seemed utterly at ease. She was anything but. "By the sound of it, you're Irish," she said, keeping her gaze trained forward.

"Sure, I was born there. I'm American, now. I spent six years there, almost twenty here. I must say you have the look of the Irish yourself."

"My mother," she said.

"Mine, too," he teased. "She's still there. I thought she might come over but, alas, losing my brothers sucked the wind from her sails. Or I suppose so. Haven't had word from her in a few years."

Astrid glanced at him. "I'm sorry."

He shrugged. "Perhaps we all have a fate. I don't know. What I do know is that chance can carry a big cudgel and wallop anyone with it."

He was certainly the cheerful sort. And gregarious. Likely, he charmed all the ladies he came across. She hoped he wasn't under the impression she would be one of them. The idea of it got her back up. It took more than a handsome face and a friendly demeanor to turn her head.

"What projects are you working on in the greenhouse?" he asked, speaking up to include the children.

"We have plants that we tend," Noemi spoke up. "I am growing parsley and carrots."

"I love carrots," he exclaimed. "Probably why my hair is red. Have you eaten any yet?"

"No. They're not big enough yet."

"I'm growing apricots," Arthur said.

"I'm growing cucumbers," Gabriel said.

"And you, Miss Astrid?"

"I have several projects," she replied evasively.

"I hope you'll show me."

She frowned as they rounded the house. "If you drove Lord and Lady Sonden, I imagine you'll be leaving soon."

"Sadly, yes. Unless I can find a job here in the meantime. Ahh, I don't mean that. No matter what, I'd drive them back. You start a job, you finish a job. Suppose I'll have to come back to look something."

Obviously, he was teasing. Or was this his idea of flirting? "It is very different than the city, I'm sure."

"Oh, for sure and certain."

"Far less opportunity."

"Far cleaner air," he said. "Not to mention less crime and less poverty."

"Poverty exists everywhere."

He grinned and nodded. "Suppose you're right. Were you born and raised here?"

"In the village. Yes."

"I'm going to run," Noemi announced.

"Me, too," Gabriel said, and the children took off before she could even respond.

She folded her arms and kept up her pace. Normally she would be glad for the children's initiative and the chance for a solo walk and a quarter hour to herself. But she wasn't alone. Zander stayed right with her, probably convinced she'd be falling at his feet before the hour was up. Piffle and Tosh to that! He did not know her.

~~~

Bertha's Novelties Shoppe was merely a section of the village's general store closed off by two walls and a colorful bead and button curtain that dangled from a rod and continued knocking together after anyone passed through.

The well-stocked general store, owned by Mr. Carlton Deevers, Jr., was a place of practicality offering goods that ranged from tools to fabric, crockery and dishes to cartridges, shells, and bullets. There were dry goods, oats, flour, sugar and more. There were tall, glass jars of candy. Bags of dry-roasted peanuts scented the air. There was a red cast iron stove in the center of the store that warmed it nicely.

The novelty shoppe was run by Mr. Deever's mother, and was her pride and joy. It was cozy with shelves of jewelry, knickknacks, and toys. On the far wall was an impressive four-level dollhouse filled with perfectly placed furniture and dolls.

Jane entered the shoppe followed by Charlotte and Theo, and introduced them to Bertha Deevers, a petite and attractive lady of perhaps sixty with a neat bun and a warm smile.

"It is a pleasure," Bertha said. "Are you ladies simply perusing my little domain or have you need for anything special?"

Theo spoke up. "I have children in mind. A girl of seven, although she seems older, and a boy of five."

"I offer quite a selection of trinkets and toys," Bertha said excitedly. "I hope you may find something to please. Look about and let me know if I may assist."

"It is a charming place," Charlotte said.

"Thank you, dear. Let me get you all a basket," Bertha said, and hurried behind the counter.

Theo made her way toward a display of yo-yo's.

"Oooh, a quoits set," Charlotte said, gravitating toward the stack of boxes. "That could be fun."

Jane followed her. Each set contained a wooden spike, rings of wood, and rings of rope. She was glad there were several boxes of the ring toss game because it would be perfect gift for the children. "I will take one of those," she said, picking one up.

Theo accepted the basket from Bertha and put the yo-yo's she'd selected inside before she moved on to look at several horse figurines, some pulling wagons or carriages.

Jane went a section of dolls. There were mature looking girls with china faces and fancy gowns, their lips and cheeks painted pink, their eyes wide and blue. There were baby dolls in bonnets and frilled neck gowns. Tiny eyelashes had been painted on the closed eyes of a sleeping infants. It stirred something deep within her.

It was possible she was with child, but it was too soon to know for certain. She did not want to get her hopes up too much, but she longed for another child. She stroked the small china hand of the baby doll before moving on.

Charlotte stood in front of the dollhouse peering in at its intricate furnishings. A clever miniaturist had created the tiny works of art, and someone had spent a good amount of time arranging them all. There was a couple having tea in what looked like a morning room. A uniformed maid dusted a banister with a feather duster. On the bottom level, a cook placed a tray of cookies on a wooden worktable in the kitchen. The details were impressive. They were fantastic.

An older man read a newspaper in the parlor while an older lady sat nearby knitting. Children played in the nursery, one writing on a chalkboard easel while the other sat on a rocking horse. There were elaborate chandeliers, tiny teacups and saucers, rugs on the floor, and stocked cupboards. Jane sidled up next to her. "Every time I'm here, the dolls are doing something different," she said quietly.

Charlotte grinned. "I would be tempted to play with it myself. Is it for sale?"

"I doubt it," Jane said just above a whisper.

Bertha came toward them carrying a small object. "Look what arrived," she said, showing them a tiny doll vase with flowers. She bent to place it on a table in the drawing room, placing it just so. "Here you are," she said softly. She straightened and admired it. "I'm expecting a baby any day. In a pram with wheels that move."

"It's really marvelous," Charlotte said.

Bertha's eyes gleamed. "Isn't it? Such a perfect little world. We should all have such a perfect little world."

When the ladies left the store, they were armed with purchases. Jane had a set of quoits for the children, Charlotte had building blocks hand-painted with forest animals for her young cousin, and Theo had gifts for her nieces and nephews, as well as Gabby and Nate. Jane linked one arm through Theo's and another through Charlotte's. It had been a delightful excursion.

~~~

The village doctor, Dr. Phineas Setterfield, was a pleasant, middle-aged man with a dramatic mustache and muttonchop sideburns. He discreetly examined Alice, sight only, no touching of an intimate nature, and was satisfied that everything seemed fine with mother and child.

Regarding the spotting, he said, "Sometimes it happens."

He recommended that she rest quietly for a few days. If no more bleeding occurred, they could travel home at a leisurely pace, stopping whenever she felt fatigued or experienced any discomfort.

When he left the room, he conferred with Nigel who'd been waiting just beyond the door. Afterwards, Nigel came in and sat facing her on the bed. She was hugging a small, crocheted pillow. "Are you alright?" he asked.

She nodded. "It really wasn't much of an examination. But he was nice."

"I'm not confident we should return home yet," Nigel said. "Perhaps not until the baby is born. Or until you're certain you feel up to it."

She was relieved he thought so, too. "I just don't want anyone else to have to change their plans," she fretted.

"I'm sure they won't. They already said most of the staff was staying behind. Of their own volition. But I'll go and speak with Joel." He leaned close and kissed her. Pulling away, he said, "We will have a healthy child," he replied huskily. "A few of them, I hope."

She placed her hands on the sides of his face. She loved him so much, she ached with it. She would have expressed it, but she could not squeeze a single word through her tight throat.

Chapter Eleven

Jane, Charlotte and Theo were dismayed to hear the news about Alice when they returned. Not only that, but Reedman dispensed it in such veiled terms that they were forced to extract the specifics bit by bit. Charlotte had an urge to take his shoulders and shake him. *Out with it, man!*

"Where is she now?" Jane asked when they had gleaned a full understanding.

"She and her sister are in the west wing drawing room. Mrs. Wahl says they are quietly engaged and … she seems well."

"Good. And the others?"

"Everyone's gathered in the salon. Convened, I should say. No, not convened. There was nothing organized about it."

"Thank you, Reedman," Jane said to spare them all further explanation.

He bowed his head and left them.

Jane turned to the others. "I'll say hello to everyone, let them know we're back and then go see her."

Theo nodded. "I'll come with you."

"Me, too," Charlotte agreed.

In the salon, Dab, Joel, JG, and Jonathan played cards in a more subdued manner than usual. Hugh sat on the floor at a table with Arthur and two other children, who must be the housekeeper's children, Charlotte realized. They were playing a board game with colorful wooden discs. She stopped to watch as Theo went to Dab, and Jane to Joel.

Nigel stood to one side of the hearth with his arms crossed watching Hugh's instruction. Charlotte could not tell if he was actually following along or too distracted by worry. His expression seemed somewhat closed off. Virgil stood next to him with a drink in hand, prattling on about some investment. How the man enjoyed his nattering. It was not the first time she'd felt a tinge of remorse that she'd brought him.

Charlotte stepped closer to Hugh and the children, and he looked up and gave her a smile that set her heart thudding like a spooked runaway stallion.

"Four, five, six," the little boy counted as he swiftly slid a disc.

"No," his sister said. "You moved too far. It's that one."

"No, it's not," he said with a frown.

"You were here, correct?" Hugh asked.

The little boy nodded.

"The thing to do is make the piece touch each square as you count it. Let's try it again. One, two, three—" Hugh counted with the boy, who ended up on the space his sister had indicated.

"Told you," she said smugly.

"That's where I was," he informed her. He stuck out his tongue at her.

"None of that, now," Hugh said lightly. "Especially when it's my turn." He picked up a pair of dice and shook it dramatically over one shoulder and then the other before dropping it with a flourish. The children laughed and mimicked him, their spat forgotten.

Someone touched Charlotte's arm, and she started. Jane and Theo were waiting on her. Talk about conspicuous! She felt herself flush as she followed them from the room. A ridiculous surge of emotion was rising in her, punishing her face, and tightening her chest. What in the world was wrong with her? Good gracious, he'd simply been playing a game with children.

But she was leaving in the morning. And she liked him so much. She might not have this opportunity again.

Opportunity?

What nonsense. What opportunity? What could she do? But what if the next time she saw him, he was engaged or he'd joined the clergy or—

Jane handed her a hanky. Charlotte drew breath to say she didn't need it when she realized a tear was snaking down her face. She swiped it away and then took the handkerchief. She would have uttered a thank you, but her throat was too tight. "I have no idea what's wrong with me," she said when she could manage it.

"There is nothing wrong with you," Theo stated emphatically.

It was the way Theo said it, and the way Jane was looking at her that made it clear they knew precisely what she was feeling. Damn it all, she was not a sixteen-year-old girl. She was more than ten years beyond it, staring spinsterhood squarely in the face. It was embarrassing to be so transparent. Of course, they were women. Hopefully none of the men could read her so clearly. How humiliating that would be.

When they reached the drawing room, Jane and Theo continued inside while Charlotte took a moment. Backing up against the wall, she took a few deep breaths and dabbed at her face. When she was ready, she straightened her shoulders, and went into the room.

Alexandria and Jocelyn sat at a table playing a card game while Alice stitched on the quilt. Jane had taken a seat next to Alice and Theo sat on Jane's far side. Charlotte walked over and sat on the other side of Alice.

"Are you alright?" Jane asked Alice solicitously.

"I hope so," Alice replied. "It frightened me."

Theo nodded. "Of course, it did. It would anyone."

Jocelyn cleared her throat lightly. "The doctor thinks everything is fine," she said casually.

"Yes," Jane replied with a smile. "We heard. Thank heaven."

"We've been sharing stories to keep Ali from fretting too much. Jane, we heard about the dog you smuggled in and kept as a girl."

"The dog she kept smuggling in," Alexandria corrected. "Despite our mother refusing to allow it."

Jane harrumphed. "I'll have you know, most of the staff became my conspirators. Even Alexandria helped out a time or two."

"On the condition our mother would not be told of my involvement," Alexandria interjected. "I have always known who buttered my bread."

Charlotte chuckled at her candor.

"Did you get to keep the dog?" Theo asked Jane.

"Yes. On the condition that Mamma never had to see or smell or hear the dog again, which included any damage the little beast might do. Those were her words."

"It helped that our father was on Jane's side," Alexandria said.

"He adored Jezzie," Jane proclaimed. "She ended up being more his dog than mine. I even caught Mama with the little beast curled in her lap a time or two."

Charlotte grinned. "Sometimes we don't know what we want until it's whining and nudging us to be petted."

Jocelyn laughed. "Well said, Charlotte."

Jane laid a hand on Alice's arm. "Anything you need, anything at all, you have only to say."

Alice took a moment to reply. "I hate to be a burden—"

"Oh, no. I will not hear that sort of talk! You have one responsibility and that is to take care of yourself and the baby. You will consider this your home for as long as you need."

Alice ducked her head and nodded. Charlotte felt like wrapping an arm around her and crying, too.

For Alice's anxiety.

For her own.

"Jane is very bossy," Alexandria spoke up. "When she knows she's in the right."

"Did you have a nice time in the village?" Jocelyn asked, determined to get them on safer, more cheerful ground.

The three agreed with alacrity. "We had a lovely time," Theo said.

"Jane," Alice said anxiously. "Did you ever have … bleeding before Arthur came?"

Jane hesitated and then shook her head.

Alice looked to Theo. "What about your sisters?"

"Not that I remember," Theo replied almost apologetically.

"I know someone who did," Charlotte offered. "A friend of our family, Bess Clayton. She was a neighbor before she got married."

Alice had turned to her, her eyes wide. Alice had one blue eye and one green. Although you got used to the sight, up close, it never failed to astonish.

"What happened?" Alice asked. "Was the baby alright?"

"Yes! Perfectly alright. I recall how the incident scared Bess, though. She woke to find blood on the back of her gown when she was perhaps seven months along. That was her first pregnancy. She's had two other children now." She paused. "Try not to worry."

"That's what I keep telling her," Jocelyn said, having turned to face them.

"Do you know if it only happened the once?" Alice persisted.

"I believe there may have been a few instances. It was never a lot of blood. And then it stopped as mysteriously as it started. The baby, Harry is his name, was a strapping baby boy with a head full of dark hair."

Alice managed a weak smile.

Jane picked up the quilt. Theo pulled some on her lap and said, "I'm ready to get to work. We'll have this done in no time."

As Alice leaned back with a sigh, Charlotte caught Jane's eye. Clearly, her old friend did not know if she had made-up Bess Clayton or not, but it was evident that it had relieved Alice's mind. Charlotte gave her a guileless smile.

~~~

It had been a day of shake ups and changes in plans, but by the time the adults gathered in the salon for aperitifs, there was a far more relaxed and even grateful atmosphere amongst them. Alice looked tranquil in a gown of blue and ivory.

The story had gone round that Charlotte knew of a lady who'd experienced something similar to Alice, and all had turned out well. Even now, it was being talked about between JG and

Jocelyn. Hugh stood near them, as did Charlotte. He had a suspicion that Charlotte had made the tale up to assuage Alice's worry. "Clayton," he murmured. "Bess Clayton." He turned to Charlotte. "Would she be the wife of Harold Clayton?"

Charlotte blinked. "Yes. Do you know them?"

He nodded. "He's a friend of my brother's. I believe they have three young sons if I'm not mistaken?"

She looked delighted. "No. The youngest is a girl. Beatrix. We see them from time to time."

"That's right," he exclaimed. "Trixie."

Charlotte nearly laughed. "Yes."

Alice was listening to it all. When the topic of conversation moved on, Hugh stepped closer to Charlotte. "What a small world it is," he commented.

"Well, London is not exactly the world," she teased.

"True. How is it you know the Claytons?"

"Bess was a neighbor of ours. Her parents still live there. Very nice people."

"Ah." Hugh shifted and spoke so only Charlotte would hear. "She has a wart right here," he said tapping the center of his chin. "Does she not?"

Charlotte nodded with a solemn expression but a twinkle in her eyes. "Of course, we don't speak of it," she said just as quietly. "And one never stares."

He murmured compassionately and tried not to laugh. He adored her. He simply adored her.

The plan for departures was discussed at dinner. Alice, Nigel and Jocelyn would remain at Manoria for the time being. JG was leaving in the morning, taking Joel's carriage in order to leave his more comfortable conveyance for Nigel, Alice, and Jocelyn who would return home when it was deemed wise.

Like JG, Charlotte and Virgil were also leaving in the morning.

Joel, Jane and Arthur would ride home with Alexandria, leaving in two or three days' time. Alexandria was impatient to go while Jane almost seemed like she was dreading it.

The rest of the company, Dab and Theo, and Jonathan and Hugh, would follow them.

"Since this is our last night together," Jonathan said. "I think we should all come up with the sagest bits of advice we know to be banked for our future children."

Everyone was agreeable.

"Lady Larrowford," Jonathan said, "mistress of Manoria, you should go first."

Jane murmured thoughtfully. "I would say ... be tempered in your response, especially when something or someone has angered you."

Dab nodded in approval. "I wish I'd always done that."

"So do I," Jane laughed. "Speaking for myself, of course. But that's the wonderful thing about advice. One's child does not have to know the parent's personal failings that led to the wisdom."

"Now, you call on someone," Jonathan suggested.

She looked at Nigel. "Papa to be?"

"That's easy," Nigel replied. "My advice is do not gamble."

"Unless it's at poker with your closest friends," Jonathan added.

"Good point," Nigel replied. "In fact, don't you owe me some money from that last game we played?"

Jonathan chortled.

Nigel gestured to Theo. "Theo?"

"Enjoy and appreciate everyone you care about as much as you possibly can," Theo offered.

Everyone nodded in concurrence, mindful that she'd lost her mother and young sister in a tragic carriage accident that she'd barely survived. JG banged on the table with his hand while Dab leaned over to kiss her cheek.

JG raised his hand. "Mine is …to never eat bean soup for supper on a night your wife may want to be amorous."

Jocelyn blushed and rolled her eyes but laughed along with everyone else.

Dab went next. "Do not judge people or situations by surface appearances or by what everyone else says."

JG banged the table again. "Well said, Adonis!"

Dab quirked a brow at him.

Jonathan peered at his twin brother with challenge in his gaze. "What say you, Lord Larrowford?"

"I agree with what everyone else has said, Lord Stewart," Joel replied.

This drew a negative response all around.

"Come on," Hugh urged. "We're sharing life lessons here."

"How's this? If you happen to be eight minutes older than your brother, be prepared to receive a lot of flak."

"You can do better than that," Dab insisted.

"Fine. Know who you are and don't let circumstances change that. Good circumstances or bad because life is likely to have plenty of both."

Jane smiled at him and nodded. His friends raised their glasses.

"I think I may have another," JG said to a resounding chorus of *no!*

Dab looked at Hugh, who hadn't offered anything yet, and noticed the meaningful glance between him and Charlotte. Or had he imagined it? Dab looked at his wife who returned his gaze with a knowing expression that spoke volumes. So he hadn't imagined it! Some sort of attraction or attachment had occurred between Hugh and Charlotte Richards. When? And how did women instinctually know things involving matters of the heart? Time and again, men were the last to figure it out.

Chapter Twelve

Tonight, Hugh didn't quite know himself as he waited in the entry hall hoping Charlotte would appear. When he could stay still no longer, he paced through the large room, frequently glancing up at the mounted heads. What would they have to say about the various things they'd witnessed? He would probably seem foolish and inconsequential to them. Then again, it was easy to feel superior when you were removed from any and all choices and could only gaze down at the blundering imperfections of a living person.

He crossed through the dining hall and went up and down the corridor. He entered the library and even tried to settle on a book, but the words were a jumble from a sheer lack of concentration. Would she show up? Surely, she would guess he'd be down here. She was leaving tomorrow. He feared he might lose his mind if he didn't learn whether she was promised to Virgil.

He reshelved the book and returned to the parlor. Bracing a hand against the mantle and staring into the flames, he decided that if she did not show up tonight, he would speak with her before she left. He would say how much he'd enjoyed spending time with her and hoped they would meet again soon in the city – and he would say it in such a direct manner that his meaning was clear.

He could write her a letter tonight. He could give it some thought and express precisely what he wanted to. He wouldn't be able to slip it under her door because he didn't know which room was hers. He only knew she was staying in the family wing. He could get it to her tomorrow, but how foolish would he look if she had an understanding with Virgil? He would make it awkward for himself and for her.

"You look deep in thought," she said from the doorway.

A smile burst from him which he barely managed to dim before he turned to face her. "To be honest, I was hoping you would join me. And I was hoping it rather profoundly."

She smiled and came further into the room. "My time here has gone so quickly."

"Too quickly. Although, I'm sure you're looking forward to seeing your cousin and her family."

"I am," she replied with some reticence. "I just wish I'd planned on a few more days here."

She'd stopped a few feet from him. She looked so beautiful. So classically beautiful. How odd that he hadn't realized her loveliness before the last few days. "Before long, we'll be back in the city," he ventured. He was going to do it. He was going to declare his wish to see her there.

"What will you do?" she asked gently.

The question stymied him for a moment. "With my life? I don't know. I've been so happily distracted here, I haven't given it a bit of thought." She sat on one end of the settee, so he took the seat in the chair beside her. He was close enough that he could lean forward and touch her.

"I imagine being happily distracted was precisely what you needed," she mused.

Conversation flowed so easily between them, which was a wonderful thing, except when he had a specific topic he wanted to discuss. "I'm thankful for my time here for many reasons," he said. "Seeing this place was a delight. Being with my friends is always enjoyable, and I truly like each of their wives or soon to be wives."

"So do I," she agreed. "Theo and I have made plans to have lunch next month."

Ah! It was the perfect opening. All he had to do was ask if she would be interested in having lunch with him. Or dinner. Or a ride through the park. She would say yes or she would say no and he would have his answer. He drew breath but hesitated. He would have his answer, but what if it was the one he did not want?

"Are you alright?" she asked.

"Yes. I was just wondering—"

Her full attention was on him. *Oh Lord.* Had he simply imagined her interest in him?

"Hugh? What is it?"

Get on with it, man! It's only your cursed pride at risk. There had to be a way to smoothly ease into the subject. How? She was waiting. He felt the pressure mounting. "Are you engaged?" he blurted.

Her jaw dropped.

He felt a rush of embarrassment. Smooth indeed! But he'd gone this far. "Or engaged to be engaged?"

"What?" she breathed.

Damn! He had offended her. Had he offended her?

"Of course, I am not engaged. Or engaged to be engaged …which seems a preposterous notion to me. If two people want to be engaged, why would they simply not be?"

The more she went on, the more frustrated she became and the deeper she blushed, the better he felt. She was wonderful. Plainspoken, truthful, intelligent, adorable and wonderful.

"To whom, for Goodness' sake? To whom would I be engaged?" She huffed. "Do you think I am a dishonest person? Yes, I did tell a fib about Bess Clayton, but—"

He reached over and took hold of her hand, which silenced her. "So did I," he said. "My brother is not actually friends with George Clayton."

"Harold," she corrected. "His name is Harold."

"Right. Harold. Of course, I do not think you dishonest. You are nothing but honest." He cringed. "I didn't mean that exactly. You are a great deal more than honest but … what I meant to say, what I want to say is that I want to see you, Charlotte. When we get back to the city. I want to take you to lunch and to dinner. To whatever amusements you like. I want to escort you to parties and take rides with you through the park. I want to get to know your parents and have you get to know my family." He paused to give her a chance to speak, but now she merely watched him with soulful eyes. Big, brown, beautiful, soulful eyes. "I am without employment or a specific direction at the moment, but I am not destitute."

She looked solemn. "I never thought you were," she said with a shake of her head.

"I will figure out the right direction."

"I'm certain you will!"

"I have relished every moment in your company."

Tears shone in her eyes as she nodded. "And I yours."

"Is that a yes to us seeing one another … to courting once we're home?"

Her fingers tightened around his and she nodded rapidly. She smiled and then laughed. "Yes!"

He felt a heady rush of joy – until she suddenly looked aggravated and yanked her hand away.

"But why did you ask if I was engaged?" she snapped. "What put the notion in your head?"

He hesitated a moment. "It was something Virgil said."

She seemed confused. "What did he say?"

"Basically, that you were."

"He inferred I was engaged?"

"That you were engaged to one another," he said carefully. Anger instantly rose within her, stiffening her limbs. He could see it. He would never have to guess when she was angry with him.

"What exactly did he say?"

"Would you care for a drink?" he hedged.

"No, I would not. What did he say?"

He let go of her hand and leaned back. "It was a few nights ago when we were playing individual games. We were playing pinochle, he and I and Dab and Alexandria."

One of her brows lifted. "I recall. She was stealing glances at you with an adoring expression."

"Yes," he admitted. "I thought it very odd. Anyway, Virgil commented on the number of married couples and engaged couples amongst us. It seemed an offhanded comment. Then Dab remarked, tongue in cheek, that Jonathan and Lakely were more engaged to be engaged. I think you know about them?"

"Yes," she said curtly. "Go on."

"Then Virgil said something to the effect of … it was the same with him. I believe his statement was, then that makes two of us. Meaning engaged to be engaged."

She folded her arms, her face a mask of displeasure.

"Dab offered congratulations," he continued. "He asked if the lady was anyone we knew. Virgil seemed puzzled by the query and then he looked at you. It was so direct a look, I said, 'Charlotte?' I swear, it was an involuntary response; I was so taken aback."

She exhaled and looked away.

"He was immediately regretful that he'd spoken," he added. "He asked that we not say anything because you were a private person, and nothing was official yet."

"Official," she muttered. She looked back at him. "But why didn't you say something? We've spoken privately since then."

"I wanted to. You can't know how I've wanted to. But we kept getting interrupted before I could." He realized he'd gotten the answer he wanted about the engagement, but now the mood between them had changed. "I know this has taken you by surprise—"

"Yes. It has. I feel hurt by it. Betrayed. Virgil is the closest thing to a brother that I have. That he would claim—" She looked away sharply and then dabbed at her eyes.

"Had he ever suggested such a thing?"

She sighed and looked back at him. "More than suggested, he proposed the idea. Naturally, I shut it down. I thought we were done with it but, on the way here, he brought it up again."

"Oh?"

She nodded. "He begged for two minutes to make his case and I gave it to him. Before explaining in no uncertain terms why the answer was and would always be no. I could never feel that way about him. I told him I would rather be a spinster than to marry without love. He maintains that romantic love is a fleeting and unimportant thing. I do not agree."

"Nor do I."

"But I never veered from my position. Not once. Not for a single moment. I can assure you, there is no question in his mind as to where I stand on the subject. So to say or suggest what he did was a … well, blatant lie."

Hugh came and sat beside her. He took hold of her hand again, which felt like a privilege. She had long, slender fingers. "I am so happy for it," he admitted. "In telling you, I made you unhappy. But in telling me, you've made me happier and more relieved that I can say." She gave him a whisper of a smile and he leaned closer and kissed her cheek. She smelled of warmth and soap and lily of the valley.

She shifted more toward him. "I am not unhappy. Not with you. In fact, I'm very happy in this moment."

"I'm so glad. I've been afraid I might have imagined the feelings between us. Not on my end, of course."

"I have wondered the same thing. It is not common practice for a wonderful, handsome man to have feelings for the likes of me."

He nearly laughed. "The likes of you? There is none. You, Charlotte, are one-of-a-kind. But did you say wonderful and handsome? Could we go back to that part?"

"Wonderful and handsome and kind and intelligent and excellent at explaining games to children."

Her expression was so loving, he couldn't speak for a moment. Now that he'd seen it, now that he knew her, he could not imagine considering any other woman to be his wife. "Miss Charlotte Richards, this may be untoward, but … I want to say, to pledge, that will cherish you if you allow it."

A shaky sigh escaped her. "Perhaps you should kiss me," she uttered, "—and then I will decide if I will allow it."

It felt as though he'd been waiting his entire life for this moment. He leaned in and touched his lips to hers so softly, the contact tickled. Pressing deeper and closer, he heard her breath catch and felt a tremor run through him. Her lips were soft and supple. Their noses, cheeks, and foreheads touched. Their breath intermingled. He had kissed women before, but he did not recall ever experiencing this feeling of raw intimacy that made him ravenous for more.

She made a soft moan and then drew back, embarrassed by it. She smiled. "Your mustache," she said.

"It will be gone tomorrow."

"No, I do not dislike it. I'm just ... nervous I suppose. I'm sorry."

Sorry? She was the most lovely, gracious woman in the world, and he wanted her desperately. He was about to try again when she pressed her lips to his. Her fingers, those fabulous fingers, traveled up the back of his neck and raked through his hair as her lips parted sweetly in an invitation he was eager to accept.

Ah! The taste of her. There was an undertow between them, and dizzying, eddying currents of desire and awareness and deep, carnal need. His grip tightened around her as she leaned into him wanting him as much as he wanted her.

They would make love. Not here and now but in the future and often. Their lovemaking would be fueled by passion and equality. For now, he relished her nearness and the heat and shape of her beneath his hand. It felt as though he'd been waiting his entire life for this moment, and she had been worth the wait.

~~~

Astrid was dressed in her nightgown, sitting cross-legged on the bed while darning a hole in her stocking. She hissed when the needle jabbed her finger. She glared at the offending dot of blood and popped it into her mouth. It was *his* fault, Zander's fault, that she was distracted.

There was a light rap at the door and in slipped Emilia wearing a dressing robe and carrying a jar of cream. "Will you get the center of my back?"

Astrid set her sewing aside. "Is your shoulder still bothering you?"

Emilia nodded. "I must keep sleeping on it wrong." She handed the jar over before positioning herself in front of her and lowering her robe.

Astrid set her sewing aside and dipped her fingers into the unctuous cream that smelled of gardenia. She smoothed it on Emilia's back and rubbed it in.

"That feels good," Emilia said, swaying with the application. "Why were you so preoccupied at supper?"

"Was I?"

"You know you were." After a beat of silence, she added. "Is it Zander MacShane?"

"No," Astrid snapped.

"The children told me all about him. The poor lad sounds smitten."

"The *poor lad* is all charm and flash," Astrid retorted. It wasn't true, but she didn't want to discuss it. "Here," she said handing the jar back.

Emilia's back was still gooey with the lotion, so she gathered the robe in front of her and turned to face her younger sister with a discerning expression.

"Don't go analyzing me, Emilia."

"Tell me about him."

"There's nothing to tell."

Emilia cocked her head.

"He's leaving in a day or two, so what could there be to tell? He is charming, and we had a diverting conversation. End of story." Emilia nodded in acceptance, which darkened Astrid's mood, for some reason. "He made the children laugh. He's good with children."

"That's nice." She paused. "Alice Walston had a bit of bleeding this morning. She saw it in the chamber pot. That's why they didn't leave today."

"And why the doctor was here," Astrid realized.

Emilia nodded.

"Are they still leaving tomorrow?"

"No. They will be staying at least a few more days and perhaps until the baby is born. It depends on how she's feeling."

"She probably ought to wait," Astrid murmured. She leaned back against the headboard and drew her knees up.

"I hope you know," Amelia said tenderly. "Whatever you're feeling and thinking, you're entitled to it. You needn't keep it locked inside."

Astrid turned her face away trying to ward off the sudden onslaught of tears that threatened. It wasn't a question of being entitled to her feelings, they were simply too overwhelming to make sense of. Zander had appeared out of the clear blue like her very own Prince Charming, practically declaring his undying devotion for her. Her guard had flown up, but he had stayed with her and continue talking. And talking. He'd made her smile and then laugh, and then she'd found herself slowly opening up in response to his candor.

His story had gripped her but it was the way he'd turned out that impressed her. He'd come to London as a young boy with his three elder brothers after the uprising of ninety-eight, the battle of Vinegar Hill. It was either that or risk being caught and transported to a penal colony in Australia.

His brothers all perished over the next three years from 'bad luck and bad decisions,' leaving Zander on his own. As a nine-year-old, he'd been put into an orphanage that he'd run away from. He had escaped it for the streets where The Bowery Boys, a gang of thugs and misfits claimed him as one of their own.

For years, he committed petty crimes and witnessed more violence than most people see in a lifetime, including some of his friends' necks being stretched. He finally stole away from the lair he'd called home and joined the British Navy where he'd worked as a seaman for six years.

"A lot of the others complained about the food," he said. "There was little but salt meat, hard biscuits, and sauerkraut, but when you've known the feeling of your belly hugging your back from hunger, you're thankful for it. There was no complainin' from me."

That was what moved her. Rather than feel sorry for himself, which he had good reason to do, he'd kept an optimistic heart. He knew gratitude and hope and kindness. He truly believed the perfect life was there to be found if only he kept searching and working for it.

"Astrid?" Emilia asked.

Astrid looked at her sister with a resolute sigh. "I only just met him today, so I will not make more out of it then there needs to be, but he turned my head. I will admit that much." She shrugged. "I liked him. I like him," she corrected herself. "But what does that matter when he's leaving?" If anything, it had given her a taste of something she would probably never have. Real life was not a fairy tale. He was not her Prince Charming, and she was not the beautiful princess that he seemed to see. It was nice that he saw her that way. More than nice. Perhaps it was a wonderful thing to have experienced.

Or would it just leave her aching for more?

"I don't know what the future holds any more than you do," Emilia rejoined.

"But we can be realistic," Astrid retorted. "After all we've been through, we should be the most realistic people in the world. We are not like the guests. We don't flit about from this great estate to that one with nothing to do but visit and enjoy ourselves. We don't travel to the city for the season or to attend the theatre. I wouldn't even know how to act in the city."

Emilia stood and adjusted her robe. Tying the belt, she said, "Of course, you would. You would act no differently there than you act here." She sat again. "Do you want to go? For a visit? I feel certain that could be arranged."

Astrid thought about it and then shook her head. That had never been a strong desire. "I love it here."

"As do I, but you are young, and the world offers a lot of experiences. It might be enjoyable to—"

Astrid shook her head again. What she wished is that Zander could remain close by. Then again, if wishes were horses, beggars would ride.

~~~

Dab and Theo lay facing one another after making love. A fragment of moonlight had stolen through the mostly drawn curtains to light a curl of her hair, making it gleam golden. Dab couldn't help himself; he toyed with it.

"If this place really is magic," she mused sleepily.

"Can there be any doubt? Last Christmas, I wished for you and here you are."

"I remember the story very well. You made a wish to feel more."

"And here you are. Heart of my heart."

She smiled. "Does one have to be here on Christmas Eve or Day for a wish to come true?"

"Why? Do you want to make a wish?"

"I already have."

"Are you going to share it?"

"We share everything, do we not?" She paused. "I wish for an autumn baby."

He didn't react for a moment. "You're ready, then?"

"Yes. Are you not?"

He was quiet for a few moments as he studied her. "I never imagined a love like ours. I didn't think I was cut out for it."

"You are so cut out for it," she rejoined.

"I love you," he said. "And I will love our child or children. I only hope I won't resent the attention you lavish on them."

"You won't."

He smiled. "You're always so sure of me."

"Yes. I am." She closed her eyes, ready for sleep.

It was quiet except for the crackling of the fire, a slight whistle in the chimney, and the echoey hoot of a distant owl.

"I would like to see Hugh as happy as the rest of us," he murmured.

She opened her eyes and rose up on an elbow. "I have a thought about that."

"Oh?"

She grinned. "A good one, I think."

"Do tell."

Lord Sonden/Dabney Adams

'At 6'4, with dark hair and eyes, Dab was ridiculously good looking. Few women could resist swooning, figuratively speaking, and Dab rarely failed to charm anyone if he tried. He was fully aware of the magnetism of his looks, but his handsome features were like having two hands and two feet. They were his. So what? If anything, his looks had been a detriment in his life.'

Lady Sonden/Theodora Adams (nee Martel)

'She had light brown hair with a fair amount of gold mixed in. She was pretty. Very pretty. There was a gripping innocence about her that made Lakely understand Dab's attraction.'

Chapter Thirteen

The next morning, there was a soft knock on Jocelyn's door, so quiet, in fact, she didn't know if it was intended for her. She rose from her vanity without finishing her hair. It was only half pinned in place. She opened the door to find JG standing there. It was only seven in the morning. "Good morning," she said quietly. She stepped back and waved him in, then closed the door behind him.

"I'm leaving," he said. "The driver is ready and waiting. Actually, it's the footman. He says he can drive. I really think he just wanted a vacation in the city."

She would not sulk, but – "I thought you'd go after breakfast."

"I had difficulty sleeping. Worried for Grandfather."

She nodded, understanding that. She, too, was concerned.

"So, I got up early and ate something, and Duffy packed a hamper for us."

"Oh, good. That was nice."

"It was."

She stepped close and stroked his vest with a sigh. "I hope it's a safe and speedy journey."

He took hold of her hands and clutched them chest high. "We'll be fine. Take care of Alice."

"I will."

"It's rather a frightening time, isn't it?"

"There is apprehension," she admitted. "That's only natural. We've seen our sisters go through it, but—"

He bobbed his head. "Not exactly the same as going through it yourself. Poor Nigel is as taut as an overtightened bowstring."

It was true. "Give my love to your grandfather."

"I will." He leaned in and kissed her cheek before he pulled back and looked at her. "I would never choose to leave you."

She smiled tenderly. "I know."

"Ever. Well, only in slumber, if that counts. And in the privy. And in the bath. Although—" he added with a mischievous expression.

"JG," she chided.

"No, you're right. No time for naughty talk. Must hit the road." He released a long sigh and pressed his forehead to hers. "It's true though. When the choice is mine, I will not be apart from you."

She felt the same. "Safe journey, my love."

He pulled back and nodded. "Yes, indeed. I will tell my driver your orders." He released her and started out but looked back with one last loving smile that she felt in her heart.

John George Baillie
Marquess of Blairwood

'JG would never have been considered the best-looking man in the room, unless perhaps he was the only man in the room. The heir apparent to a dukedom stood five feet ten inches tall and had ginger hair.'

Miss Jocelyn Weatherly

'Jocelyn ... possessed a simple, wholesome handsomeness. (She) was a sweet, thoughtful young woman.'

~~~

When Dab saw Charlotte leave the dining room more than an hour after everyone had finished breakfast, he suspected he would find Hugh there. "I wish you a good journey," Dab called to Charlotte.

"You, as well," she returned. "Take care of that fabulous wife of yours."

"It will be my pleasure."

She laughed. "I don't doubt that, Lord Sonden."

Grinning, Dab continued into the room to find Hugh deep in thought, his hands resting on the back of a chair. "Charlotte is a special lady," he said, rousing Hugh from his reverie.

Hugh looked at him. "Yes, she is."

"And speaking of special ladies," Dab said as he closed the distance between them. "My wife is rather brilliant."

Hugh smirked. "Because she chose to marry you?"

"Well, there is that," Dab replied with a straight face and only a modicum of strain to his facial muscles. "No. Last night, Theo suggested, and I agree, that you would be an excellent headmaster."

Hugh's smirk vanished. He blinked. "A headmaster?"

"Yes. And it just so happens that we know of a place that needs a good school. Hertford has workhouses and orphanages. What we ought to have is a quality public grammar school. It could be a day school but also a boarding school for those who need it. All student costs would be covered."

"That sounds like a worthy plan. Expensive but worthy."

"Hertford is a growing, prospering place," Dab said with a shrug. "There are people there whom, we believe, would help establish such an institution."

"I am truly flattered, but I've had no experience or training that—"

"What I'm suggesting is something new, so who would have experience at running such a school? Listen, the idea has just been hatched, so there will be a mountain of details to work out. Funding. Location. Staff. But the concept is sound."

Hugh nodded. "The idea is wonderful. Although I don't imagine the execution will be as easy as you may hope."

"I don't expect it will be easy, but I am … enthused by it. More than that. I'm motivated by it." He'd liked the idea when Theo brought it up and he liked it even more today. It felt right. His uncle, from whom he'd received a sizeable inheritance, would have wholeheartedly endorsed it for many reasons, perhaps atonement among them. It felt good to know that.

"Coming across Gabby and Nathan changed you," Hugh commented gently.

"Yes, it did. Undeniably. Come across half starved, homeless children in your backyard, and just see if it doesn't change you to the marrow of your bones. But here is the thing. The heart of the matter. You have a gift with people, bringing out the best of them. You are intuitive, loyal, protective. Not to mention wonderful with children."

Hugh seemed surprised and moved. "Thank you."

"All of that was more of an observation than a compliment, but I mean it. It makes you a very natural fit for the project." He paused. "You have been important in my life. You are important in my life." He cleared his throat, trying to rid himself of the sudden, uncomfortable lump in it. "I know you are an excellent teacher and would be equally good as headmaster. Will you give it some thought?"

"I will. Of course, I will. Thank you for thinking of me."

Dab clapped his arm before leaving the room.

~~~

Charlotte and Virgil had ridden for a quarter of an hour, and she had not said a word to him. He'd chatted, commenting on this thing or that, but mostly he watched out the window at the slow-falling snow. She knew good and well that he was aware something was amiss, and she suspected he knew exactly what it was.

In a way, she felt torn. She was aglow with thoughts and feelings for Hugh, but exasperated with Virgil. Had he said what he had because he was threatened by Hugh? Had he perceived the attraction between she and Hugh even before she had? Was Virgil that astute? She hadn't thought so, but why else would he claim they were promised to one another, especially to Hugh? Oh! And then ask to keep it secret. It had been conniving.

"I was impressed with that butler," Virgil remarked casually. "In fact, with all of Larrowford's servants. I wonder if that's indicative of this region?"

"Why did you say we were engaged?"

"What?"

She shifted to better look at him. She was done with the game playing. She wanted the truth. "Why, when you were playing pinocle, did you claim we were engaged? Or engaged to be engaged is, I believe, what you said."

He huffed in bemusement. "I don't know what you're talking about. I don't recall you and I playing pinochle."

He was being purposely obtuse. "We didn't," she replied with forced calmness. "A few evenings ago, I played a different game while you played pinochle with Miss Kingman, Dab Adams and Hugh Pritchett."

He merely raised his brows and gave a slight shrug. "If you say so. I don't especially recall that."

"I do not believe you."

"Who said that I claimed such a thing?" he challenged. "And precisely what did they say?"

She considered a moment. "What reason would Alexandria Kingman have for saying such a thing if it did not happen?"

He scoffed. "I would think her reputation for making trouble speaks for itself. Surely you read the papers last summer. Even if only half of it is true, she is a spiteful little troublemaker."

"How would claiming such a thing make trouble?" she challenged right back.

He sighed with exasperation. "Are we or are we not arguing? Obviously, it has made trouble. Besides, I am not that well acquainted with Miss Kingman to know how her tiny, little mind works."

"It wasn't her who told me," she stated coolly.

His expression changed. Hardened. "Let me guess. It was your Mr. Pritchett who's been making eyes at you since we arrived?"

The words shocked her and she felt herself flush. Hugh had not been making eyes at her, and even if he had, as if that excused telling a lie! She looked out the window and bit her tongue to keep from lashing out because her response would be anything but tempered. Yanking off her glove and clawing his face had great appeal in her imagination, but that was where it would remain. "I believe you said what you did to curb any interest he might have had in me." She looked at him accusingly. "And that hurts and angers me."

"It's been abundantly clear that you're miffed, but the silent treatment and your sulking are beneath you."

Miffed? Sulking! What was she, a mere child to be scolded for unseemly behavior? He was obfuscating everything for his own petty purposes. "What you did was mean spirited and … a betrayal."

"Oh, don't be so overdramatic. I was drinking at the time. We all were. I don't even know exactly what I said. It's possible I did say something because I didn't like the way he was looking at you." His lip curled. "I was being protective because the man is common. I didn't want him getting thoughts about you."

"He is anything but common," she retorted. "He is a gentleman."

"What am I?" he practically yelled.

"I wish you would admit that you told that lie to manipulate the situation."

His face had reddened. "I invited you on this trip. I have treated you and acquiesced to your every whim. Was that manipulation?"

He was twisting everything while evading the real subject.

"For your information, Charlotte, and for the record, nothing I said was what I believed to be a lie. I *have* asked you to marry me. I know you're not ready to consent, but I believe that you will in time."

She huffed. She could only gape at his condescension and arrogance.

"So I said something to that effect. Then, fearing I'd spoken out of turn, I asked that my confidence remain between us. That just shows you who *he* is. He couldn't wait to run and tell you, could he? He couldn't wait to stir up trouble between us."

She shook her head. She'd thought, given their history, they could have an honest conversation, but was this an honest conversation? Did he really believe what he said? He couldn't have. "You heard me say that I would never marry without being in love. You heard me tell you that I could never feel that way about you."

"I am through with this conversation," he hissed coldly.

"You don't even see where your fault lies in this, do you? You're not sorry at all."

"Oh, I'm sorry. I'm very, very sorry ... that I asked you on this trip. I am sorry that you are here and I'm listening to this drivel. I am very sorry about it."

Her jaw had grown lax, and tears stung her eyes. "Virgil," she breathed.

He scowled out the window. "Don't try to sweet talk me now. I told you, I am done with this conversation."

Sweet talk him? Good God. "We are cousins and we have been lifelong friends," she uttered shakily. "Please tread carefully that you do not destroy our friendship."

He turned his full glare on her. "Do you know what I care for our friendship?" He flung a gloved hand in the air as if shewing off a bothersome fly. "That's what I care. Friendship was fine and dandy when we were children, Charlotte. We haven't been children for quite some time. I have not wanted *friendship* between us in years. I think you know that. I think you've been using me, but now you wonder if someone better has come along. Well, I have news for you. Hugh Pritchett is not better."

"Stop," she pleaded. "Just stop."

"I made inquiries," he said bitterly. "Pritchett has no money, no house of his own, no decent prospects."

"I love him," she said quietly.

He looked as incredulous as he was livid. "Love him? You just met him a few days ago. How ludicrous is that?"

She had, in fact, *not* just met Hugh a few days ago, but this argument had gone too far. It was pointless and hurtful. "We do need to be finished with this conversation." She'd never seen this side of him, and she never wanted to again. The tension was making her stomach hurt. "I am truly sorry if I've hurt you. I never meant to do that."

"You should be sorry," he scoffed.

She stared straight ahead, battling swells of fury and frustration. It took minutes before she trusted the strength of her voice. "We cannot, must not, bring this animosity into Bridgwater," she said as evenly as possible. "Can we get beyond it for the sake of the journey and for Millie and her family?"

He sniffed. "I don't know that I can. I'm not sure I'll ever be able to get beyond it."

She shook her head slowly. She could not and would not endure this level of hostility for the remainder of the trip. She didn't deserve it. Millie didn't deserve it. "If that is really and truly how you feel, then I wish to be left behind."

"Shall we stop right here and let you out?" It was asked scathingly; the thought was so preposterous.

She swallowed. "Perhaps you'll be so good as to drop me in the village." A muscle in his jaw bulged as he seethed and stewed. She could see it and sense it out of the corner of her eye.

"Do you think I will allow you to make a fool of me? Do you think I will let him, a *nobody*, make a fool of me?"

She had looked at him without meaning to as a prickling of alarm needled her all over. "No one is making a fool of you," she uttered shakily. "I would never. Nor would he. Virgil, I swear to you, you have imagined the offence. Blown it up in your mind to be something that it's not."

He continued glowering at her until he grabbed his custom-made walking stick. For a terrible moment, she feared he would strike her with it. He looked away and hit the ceiling twice. The driver reined in the horses and opened the front window to the cab, leaning in to better hear.

"Go into the village," Virgil ordered. "My cousin wishes to leave us."

"Yes, sir," the man replied before he shut the window and snapped the reins starting them back in motion.

Charlotte sat very still. She felt so stung, it was hard to think clearly. Not in a hundred years would she have anticipated the last few minutes. Surely, he didn't believe the accusations he'd flung at her. That she'd used him? That she had essentially toyed with him until a better man came along? Tears tormented her eyes, which she would not allow him to see, so she turned her head and pushed back the curtain to stare out the window.

Neither of them spoke. It was everything she could do to control her ragged breathing so he did not know how badly shaken she was. She felt alternately cold and then hot, as if heat was rising from beneath her clothing in a desperate bid to escape.

Escape.

What would he do if he realized how weak she suddenly felt? She could see him telling the driver to push on instead of stopping. He would believe it best for her to calm herself. Or so he would claim.

Escape. She needed to escape him.

If he made a move to try and stop her, she would leap from the carriage. By God, she would do it. She might break a leg in the effort, but she would not continue on with him. Thankfully, they reached the village and the carriage pulled to a stop. The driver opened the window again to ask, "Any particular place, Miss Richards?"

They were midway up the main street near the tavern. "This is fine," she replied. The words sounded strangled to her ears. Good heavens, but she was shaking all over. Now that her departure was in sight, she hated to leave things like this. She looked at her cousin who was doing an excellent imitation of a stone-faced monolith. What could she possibly say? For that matter, what could he possibly say? That he was sorry? He did not look sorry. He looked furious and insulted.

The driver opened the door, which was a relief, and offered a hand. She accepted and he assisted her out. She hoped the difficulty of the task because of the stiffness of her limbs was not obvious. She saw that he'd already removed her trunk from the back.

He shut the door behind her. "Where shall I take it, Miss?"

She glanced down the street at a loss. "The Inn," she replied weakly. "Please."

He picked it up and started toward the Inn, three doors down.

She hesitated, but what else could she say or do? She lifted the hem of her skirt and followed the driver, wondering if Virgil would call to her. Would he try to take it all back and apologize? Or make a scene? Insist she get back into the carriage?

She reached the door of the quaint inn and stretched out a hand for the brass doorknob, hesitating just a moment as she wondered if he was watching her. She had to resist the urge to glance back. She straightened her shoulders and stepped inside.

The warmth of the interior felt good and yet it hardly reached her; she was so dazed. The driver had set her trunk down and now tipped his hat to her. She nodded to him, but before she could utter her thanks, he'd hurried on.

The proprietor of the inn, a middle-aged man, stood behind the front desk with an expectant smile. It was with a sense of horror that she realized a tear was snaking down her face. She turned sharply and wiped it away. She had to go say something to him, but she doubted the strength of her own voice, and her knees did not feel altogether right either.

The innkeeper, Francis Willoughby, looked at his wife, Gloria, as she appeared with a tea tray from the kitchen at that very moment. The two of them took tea every day at this time of morning. Generally speaking, it was after guests had checked out and before any new ones checked in.

It was not as though the inn was a thriving business. On a busy week, they might have a half dozen customers, but they made do just fine. The top floor held their rooms and the bedchambers of their children. He wasn't a man who cared about prosperity. As far as he was concerned, theirs was an ideal life.

Gloria noticed the lady who had walked in. She looked at him questioningly, and he gave a quick shrug and a significant bob of his head toward the lady. She walked around the counter with the tray. She stopped even with her and saw the stricken look on her face.

"Good morning. Will you sit and have a cup of tea?" Without waiting for a reply, Gloria went to one of the three small tables, each with a spotless tablecloth, and set down the tray. "This has a nice view of both the fire and the falling snow."

"Thank you," the lady replied. She came and sat.

Gloria poured tea for her. "Have you just arrived?"

"No. I've been at Manoria."

"A wonderful place. Have you enjoyed it?"

"Very much. I left this morning and—"

Gloria's heart went out to the lady as her voice caught. Clearly something had occurred that had greatly disturbed her.

"I will need a ride back," the lady stammered. "I can pay for it, of course. Can you suggest someone who might take me?"

"Take you back to Manoria?" Gloria asked to be certain.

The lady nodded.

"Certainly. Why, I would think someone was already heading that way. The grocers or Mister Kerr, perhaps. He's Lord Larrowford's man of business. Or my husband could drive you."

The lady sighed with relief. "Thank you. You're very kind."

"Not at all. There is no one in the village who isn't grateful to Lord and Lady Larrowford. They are so generous. You enjoy your tea, Miss—"

"Richards. Charlotte Richards."

"I'm Gloria Willoughby. My husband and I are the proprietors."

"It's a pleasure, Mrs. Willoughby," Charlotte Richards said.

"The pleasure is mine, Miss Richards. I'll have some gingerbread out of the oven soon and I'll bring you a piece." She started back to her husband only then realizing she'd left the second cup on the tray. Oh, well. It was of no consequence.

Charlotte felt more in control of her faculties even before she had fixed her tea and taken a drink. A fire blazed merrily and noisily in the hearth, and the snowfall seemed a protective curtain from the various hurts of the world. She hated the way things had gone with Virgil, but she hadn't said a single thing that she didn't mean.

And now? She would do her best to put it behind her. She would return to Manoria and then ride back to the city with one of the others who were leaving tomorrow. She sighed as she leaned back in the chair. Some of her tension was released, given that she had a clear plan in mind. And Virgil was gone. Thank God.

Except for the last half hour, her stay at Manoria had been nothing short of magnificent. It would be forever etched in her mind and heart. Not seeing Millie was a disappointment, but her cousin would understand. There was some shakiness in Charlotte's core and a slight tremor in her hands because she was not used to confrontation. It took a rather dreadful toll. But she was fine. She would be fine.

~~~

Hugh was experiencing a lightness of being he had not felt in years. A bond had formed between Charlotte and himself, and now Dab had offered a situation that felt more appealing by the moment. To head up a school for children who needed both the education and guidance? He could see it! And with Charlotte by his side? It felt so right, it almost scared him. He didn't want to get his hopes up too high in case the idea fell apart, but it felt so right.

He'd come into the village because he hadn't yet been. Larrowford was as picturesque as he'd heard, especially as snow tumbled. He strolled, glancing into the various establishments.

In the window of the dressmaker's shop, a mannequin wore a velvet gown in a dark bluish green. He pictured Charlotte in it and smiled, lit from a special inner warmth.

He went into Kixmiller's, a shoppe offering tobaccos, spices, coffee, teas and the like. It was an intriguing place with highly polished wood and the scent of pipe tobacco and rich coffee lingering in the air. He purchased packets of Turkish coffee for his friends and pipe tobacco for his father.

Mister Frederick Kixmiller suggested that bars of bittersweet chocolate made excellent gifts. They were delicious with coffee, or they could be made into a cup of chocolate. Very beneficial for the health, Kixmiller maintained. Hugh purchased five of them before leaving.

He passed an inn, peering in the bowed window, and then halted with a gasp to see Charlotte perfectly framed in one of the frosting panes. His jaw went lax – and then she saw him, and her reaction was no less surprised. He hurried inside, his gaze not leaving her face. Her expression conveyed relief and happiness.

"How are you here?" he stammered. He looked around but didn't see Virgil. He noticed her trunk.

"We had an altercation," she admitted.

Oh, no.

"Sit, please," she beckoned.

He sat. "Was it about what he said?"

She nodded. "I had to address it."

She seemed fragile. "Are you alright?"

"I am better now," she replied with a weak smile. "I couldn't continue on with him because he refused to assure me that he would be civil. Not for the sake of the journey or for Millie and her family. I couldn't do that to them."

The statement was baffling. "Civil? You're saying he was angry?"

"Yes. Very. He claimed what he told you wasn't so much of a lie since he had asked me, and he thought I would eventually consent."

Hugh's jaw tightened. What poppycock, but he wouldn't say so.

"I'm still absurdly close to tears over it." She inhaled and exhaled. "Oh, Hugh, I was looking at him and listening to him accuse me, and it was as if I didn't know him at all. How is that possible when I've known him all my life?"

He cocked his head. "Accusing you of what?"

She hesitated. "Of using him until someone better came along," she replied sheepishly.

"Oh, Charlotte. What rubbish!"

She glanced down, having blushed hotly. "Yes."

"I'm sure he didn't really mean it," he said soothingly. "I imagine he was lashing out because he was embarrassed to be caught out."

"That is possible, I know it is, but it doesn't make it any better. I don't know how he and I will be able to move on from this. And now I must throw myself on the mercy of my new friends to get back home."

He slowly grinned. "I cannot claim that I mind that part."

She heaved a small sigh and smiled.

"I can assure you that none of us mind giving you a ride home. Quite the opposite."

"I could not believe my eyes when I looked up and saw you. For a moment, I thought I had imagined you standing there."

He nodded. "The same thought occurred to me."

At the front desk, Francis and Gloria stood side by side, entranced by the scene before them. "It's not every day we enjoy tea and a show," he said under his breath.

"Be discreet," she urged.

He gave her a sly look. "I am. *You* be discreet."

She playfully elbowed him, and he elbowed right back. "It does make you curious, doesn't it?" she asked softly. "I wonder what happened."

"Yes. I wonder, too." He realized how silly it was to worry about discretion when the couple at the table didn't have eyes or ears for anyone but one another.

Chapter Fourteen

Alice carefully made her way down to the ground floor. It housed the kitchens, which were filled with activity. A young maid directed her to the stillroom where Jane sat at a worktable putting ingredients into small cotton drawstring bags for sachets.

Jane looked up with a smile. "Hello."

"So, this is the stillroom," Alice marveled as she looked around.

"It is. Come in."

Bundles of dried herbs hung from a rack, a hearth dominated one wall, and a ceramic still stood in the corner. The many shelves and cubicles on the longest wall held jars, canisters, baskets and bags. "I see why you like it so."

Jane nodded. "It's my favorite room, not counting the conservatory. I get utterly lost in making and growing things."

"May I look around?"

"Of course."

Alice kept one hand on her protruding middle as she circuited the room. There were small jars of spices, and larger jars of honey, jams, molasses, and dried fruit. There were carefully labeled clear glass bottles with colorful liquids. She leaned closer to read them. Lavender water. Rose water. In green bottles with larger labels were medicines. Laudanum. Paregoric. Chloride of Morphine. Alice experienced a shiver. Morphine was the medication that had nearly killed JG a year ago.

She meandered on. There were baskets of candles, bottles of wine, jugs of beer and mead and perry. There were powders and oils. There were canisters of soap and bars of soap. It all created a fascinating fusion of scents.

"So many hands have labored on what is collected here," Jane mused. "I feel the echo of their care here."

It was a lovely thought.

"How are you feeling?" Jane asked.

"I feel well, but a bit like an insect trapped under a glass."

Jane shifted to look at her with an amused grin.

"A very large insect. Nigel and Jaus keep watching me while pretending that they aren't doing it and that they have no concern at all. That's one reason I escaped here."

"That's understandable."

Alice picked up a bar of soap and smelled it.

"Are you writing much these days?"

"No." Alice set the soap down. "I finished the book, so the only writing I've been doing recently is to publishers. Unfortunately, there has been no interest. It's too sentimental, they say."

"Hmm. What do the female publishers say?"

Alice looked at her sharply before realizing Jane was jesting. "I wish there were female publishers."

"In case you were wondering, that glorious scent in the air is Mrs. Duffy's jam tarts. They'll be served with tea when they're ready."

Alice went to the table. "May I help with this?"

"Certainly."

Alice looked over the piles of dried flowers and herbs as she sat.

"For sleep aids, I pull from this pile," Jane said. "They're hops. These are dried violets, lavender, and rose petals, of course, but I use those sparingly. Rose is not my favorite scent. These are vanilla bean, which is a wonderful scent."

"Are there scents to alleviate anxiety?"

Jane nodded. "The very same. Hops, lavender." She rose and went to a basket to remove one of the completed sachets inside. "I also like this one," she said, handing it over. "Crunch it up a little and then smell it."

Alice did. "Pine," she detected. She cocked her head. "Is that a bit of cedar?"

91

Jane nodded.

Alice concentrated on the complex aroma. "There is something else. Cloves?"

"Indeed. Aromas of a magical forest."

"It's nice." Alice offered it back.

"It's yours." She sat again. "It's enjoyable to experiment with them."

Alice picked up a pinch of the hops and smelled it. She detected a vague scent of berries, freshly mown grass and perhaps the slight tang of orange. It was very pleasant. "What time will you leave tomorrow?"

Jane looked up at her. "We're not going." Alice drew a breath to object, but Jane held up a hand. "Arthur is going, riding with Alexandria. It was for his sake that we were making the trip in the first place. Because he wants to see his grandparents. The Lloyds' have wonderful traditions that he loves sharing in. Now, I know you don't want us to change a single plan that we made, but it is my preference to stay. And Joel feels the same."

Alice was at a loss for words. She couldn't help feeling guilty, but Jane seemed in earnest.

"We'll go collect him in a few weeks and visit with everyone," Jane concluded.

A maid appeared at the door with a tray of tea and pastries. "I come bearing tarts," she announced.

"Thank you, Clarice," Jane said. She cleared a space for the tray.

"It may be her best batch ever," Clarice said as she set it down.

"Ooh, that is saying something."

Alice watched the young maid sweep out. She had noticed and been impressed with the ease of the servants. Clearly, they were happy here. She and Jane fixed their tea and selected a tart. There was apricot or raspberry to choose from. Alice chose a berry tart, and it tasted as delicious as it smelled. She leaned back in her chair. What a cozy, relaxing room this was. They felt quite hidden away. "Do you miss the city?" she asked curiously.

"No," Jane replied without hesitation. "That's not to say that I don't enjoy visiting. But no. Our lives are so rich and full here." She paused, her gaze astute. "I sense that something is bothering you. May I help?"

Alice did need to confess. It was the real reason she'd sought Jane out. "I am worried that something is wrong with the baby." She swallowed. "There is hardly any movement," she whispered.

"That happens when your time draws near," Jane soothed. "The baby has grown larger and so there's less room. That's all it is."

"I once wished the baby would stop kicking," Alice admitted brokenly.

Jane gave her a tender smile. "There are few mothers who can't say the same."

Alice knew, or at least hoped, she was probably being silly, but she couldn't help it.

"The doctor thought everything was fine," Jane reminded her.

"What if he was just saying that to make me feel better?"

Jane sipped her tea. "There was a wonderful midwife in the village until last year when she passed. I never met her. It was before I came here. Her youngest daughter was her assistant and I understand she is quite competent in her own right. The reason I tell you is she now lives here."

Alice's breath hitched. "Who?"

"Mrs. Wahl's sister, Astrid. She came along to help with the children. I believe the initial thought was that we would want to keep the little ones shut away from the rest of us, which is the very last thing we want."

"That would have been before they knew you or Arthur."

"Or Joel," Jane said. "He and I met Mrs. Wahl at the same time. Of course, I was meeting everyone. He'd been here at Christmas and did not care for the housekeeper they had. She was the bitter, judgmental sort."

"Ah." Alice murmured.

"Why don't we have Astrid take a look at you?" Jane suggested. "It cannot hurt and it might make you feel better."

Alice agreed. "I'd like that. Although no one else needs to know. I don't want to worry Nigel any more than he already is. Or Jaus."

"That shouldn't be difficult to arrange."

Alice's anxiety eased a bit.

"How far along are you?"

"I don't know precisely, but I thought I would be having the baby in a month or so."

"When did you last bleed?" Jane asked softly.

Alice shrugged lightly. "The spring."

"What month?"

Alice cringed slightly with embarrassment. "I have tried to pin it down, but my monthly occurrence had not been regular for some time. Since I left London to return home."

Jane canted her head. "A year and a half ago?"

Alice nodded. "You see, I was terribly upset when I left, and my mindset did not improve once I realized I was probably in the wrong. Do you know the story?"

"I heard about how you and Nigel met and fell in love. It was significant because he was the first of them."

Alice smiled. "Yes."

"And I know there was some confusion on your part regarding Nigel's feelings. There was a misunderstanding between the two of you, a rather severe misunderstanding, and you returned home. He followed and the two of you were married in Boston before returning home."

"None of that is wrong," Alice said guardedly.

Jane leaned forward to refill their cups. "In my experience, women tell stories far better than men. I would love to hear it from your perspective."

Alice thought about it as she stirred sugar into her cup. "London was only supposed to be a visit from spring to summer, to spend time with my father's family. My granny, Aunt Julia and my cousin, Jeremy whom you've met."

Jane nodded.

"Jaus and I had never been abroad or experienced London's famed season. Our elder sisters had come with my parents years before, and now it was our turn."

"Is it much different from Boston?"

"The accents are certainly different," Alice teased.

Jane laughed as she reached for another tart.

"Yes. Many things are different." She nibbled on her tart. "When we went to Lord and Lady Merton's for dinner, perhaps a week after we'd arrived, I thought we were simply visiting an old school friend of my father's. I had no idea there had been discourse between Lord Merton and Papa regarding a potential match between Nigel and myself. It became clear that evening ... and I cannot say that I handled it gracefully."

Jane covered her mouth with the backs of her fingers as she chuckled.

Alice reached for another tart, apricot this time. "Maneuvering an advantageous match would have been something I expected of my mother, not my father." She tasted the tart. "These are delicious," she commented.

Jane nodded. "I could eat them daily. But go on."

"I was *livid* with my parents as we rode home that night. I'd actually liked Lord and Lady Merton and their grown children."

Jane's eyes twinkled. "Even Nigel?"

Alice smirked. "Even him. But there is something about being told you *should* do something for your own best interest that makes me want to dig my heels in and do the opposite thing."

"Indeed," Jane concurred.

"The first ball we attended was ... momentous. Nigel and I both had to admit to ourselves that there was a definite attraction between us. Also, Jocelyn met JG that night. And, thirdly, I clapped eyes on a lady named Therese St. Clair as she conversed with Nigel. Do you know who she is?"

"I don't believe so, but remember I was outside polite society for years. Last year's Christmas Cotillion was the first event I had attended in more than five years. Once Arthur came into the world, he was my sole focus."

Alice recalled as much. "Well, Therese St. Clair is beautiful and elegant. She is cultured and British. As she and Nigel conversed, I saw that she was in love with him. His back was turned to me so I could not see his reaction but hers was clear. I was standing next to Lakely at the time, so I asked her if there was an understanding between Nigel and Miss St. Clair. Lakely suggested that one might have developed had I not shown up. She didn't say it in those words, but that was the gist."

"I see."

"I had just met him so I couldn't ask him about it. But the doubt that it caused in me, believing that I had interfered with a courtship between them, stayed with me and ultimately wreaked havoc. What I didn't realize was that the worry and doubt that I felt, because no lady wants to be second choice, was apparent enough to Nigel that it caused him to keep an arm's length distance between us. He thought I was less than enthusiastic about pursuing a courtship with him."

"Oh, my," Jane breathed.

"Despite it all, we fell in love. Then came the calamity of the last night that we spent in London." She shook her head. "Looking back on it, it's as if every possible thing conspired against us to create the most dreadful suspicions and assumptions. For both of us. Oh, and for Jaus, too. Things fell apart for her that night, as well."

"I shall need more details," Jane said fervently.

Although the night of the *Le Grand Ball* had been traumatic, retelling it was not. Alice could now view it from a distance as if watching a play. The Alice of that night felt like a character, one she wished she could reach out and grab hold of and talk sense to. She dipped her fingers in the bowl of warm water and wiped them on a napkin.

"It was the first of July, but before I tell you the events of that night, I should explain a few other important factors. The first is that since Lord Merton had made his terrible blunder with gambling and losing, he had sworn off of it. *Sworn*."

Jane nodded.

"The second is that when we were readying ourselves for the ball that evening, my mother came into our room looking upset. She had received a letter from my sister. There are four of us, Clara, Sofia, me, and Jocelyn. She had just learned that Sophia had gone into childbirth early, had the child, a girl, and that she and the baby were both struggling."

Jane leaned forward with a worried frown. "That's why you've been so concerned, isn't it?"

Alice nodded. "In large part. Either or both of them could have died. They didn't. They're both well but yes. It weighs on me. I can't help wondering if I should have been lying in bed at home instead of traveling and visiting and having a wonderful time these last months."

"I believe the answer to that is no," Jane stated. "There is no reason for a healthy mother-to-be to behave like an invalid. But go on with the story."

"Mama told us that they were returning home in the morning, but that Jaus and I were being allowed to remain in the city as we had planned to do. Aunt Julia would be our escort."

Jane finished her last bite of tart without looking away from Alice.

"Aunt Julia went to the ball with us that evening. That fateful evening." A smile quirked on Jane's lips at the dramatic touch, which was all the encouragement Alice needed. "It was crowded and exceedingly warm, but the ballroom at Roxon Hall was enormous. There was a balcony above it and guests were everywhere. I had come off the floor after dancing when I saw Lakely. I knew she had news because she was so animated. She was trembling. I had been standing with Nigel and some of the others earlier, but I didn't see them when Lakely found me. She was looking for Ada to give her the news."

"The news," Jane repeated.

Alice nodded. "Despite her father's pledge not to gamble again, he had. And he'd *won*. He had won such a significant amount that their debts had been eliminated."

Jane huffed softly.

"Lakely wanted to share the news since Ada would no longer be forced to marry Mr. Bower." Jane frowned and drew breath to object, but Alice beat her to it. "Yes, the notion is absurd. Ada and Harrison were mad for one another, but Lakely was blind with protectiveness for her younger sister. So, she rushed off to find her … and I suddenly felt such fear and doubt all over again. Ada and Harrison loved one another, but what about Nigel? If all debts of honor had been cleared, and they no longer needed the dowry my father had promised, would that change his feelings?"

Jane was captivated.

"I looked around and saw him speaking with his father," Alice continued. "Nigel's back was to me, but I knew that he was being told the news at that very instant. Oh, Jane. It was as though everything began moving slowly. Other than my heart. Lord Merton was joyous. He motioned to an attendant for glasses of champagne. Lord Merton took one and Nigel took *two*. I couldn't breathe. He didn't yet see me and then people crowded in between us. I wanted that glass of champagne to be for me," she said longingly.

"Of course!"

"When the path cleared and I could see him again … by then I was making my way toward him … he was standing with Therese St. Clair. She had the other glass. They were toasting."

Jane's jaw dropped. "No."

Alice stuck a hand in the air. "I'll explain things from my standpoint first and then I'll describe it from Nigel's."

"You poor thing," Jane uttered, unable to restrain herself.

"It was dreadful," Alice conceded with a nod. "For a moment, or several, I was too lightheaded to move. I felt so foolish and humiliated! I had no idea then, but Ada was in the balcony watching everything unfold. She said it was like watching a horrible carriage collision and not being able to do a thing to stop it." Alice paused and took a drink. Reliving the experience was affecting her more than she thought it would. "I turned and walked away numb, dizzy, … stupefied."

"I can imagine," Jane empathized.

"I needed air. I went to the foyer. I suppose I was leaving, and then Dab walked inside after taking a smoke. He said I looked dreadful. Truthfully, I don't recall it perfectly, but I told him that things were over between Nigel and myself. That he loved someone else. At least, that's what I meant to say. What I thought I said."

Jane cocked her head, a puzzled look on her face.

Alice gave her a weak smile. "You have to understand, there is what I experienced, what Nigel experienced, and then there is the real and complete picture from the input of everyone's perspective. We've been able to dissect and understand it, but that night there was nothing but the agonizing feelings of betrayal and hurt."

"What did you do?"

"I was speaking to Dab when Nigel appeared with two glasses of champagne in his hand and a strange expression on his face. The sight of those glasses was insulting! I saw who he had chosen to celebrate the news with, so what were we drinking to now? Dab walked away, of course, and Nigel handed me the glass." She released a shaky breath.

"You needn't tell me if it's upsetting."

"No, it's fine. I felt the distance between us keenly at that point. I knew he didn't truly love me. He loved Miss St. Clair. So I helped expedite matters. I informed him I knew the news about his father." She swallowed. "In a matter of a few moments, a few sentences, we had ended things between us and I left."

"Left?"

Alice nodded. "I left. I began walking. I don't know how long I walked, or where I went. I finally hailed a cab and went home. I was numb. I couldn't feel anything."

Tears had filled Jane's eyes.

"My parents were already going home, and I was going with them. There was no point in staying. By then, Jocelyn and JG had an understanding, so she would stay. I went to her in the morning to explain I was leaving. She seemed pale and sick; I assumed from too much champagne. But then she said she was leaving too, that it was over between JG and herself."

"What?" Jane asked under her breath.

"We had no time to work anything out because we had to get to the ship on time. My mother was not missing the departure." She sighed. "It's nearly impossible to convey how blunted we both were. Jaus was every as devastated as I was, but I had no idea why and she had no idea what had happened with Nigel. All of it came out as we voyaged home."

Jane shook her head in astonishment. "I knew there had been a misunderstanding between you and Nigel, but I had no idea of the depth of it. What had gone wrong with Jocelyn and JG? It's hard to imagine anything could come between them. Or between you and Nigel for that matter, although I still have to hear events from his point of view."

"You did know that JG's grandfather, the esteemed Lord Morguston, once drugged JG's wine to keep him home from a ball?"

"Yes! And he nearly died from it."

Alice nodded. "It was that night."

Jane huffed.

"So JG did not show up, as Jaus expected, but Lord Morguston did and he and Jocelyn had a most unpleasant encounter. He said he would disinherit JG if the two of them married. He claimed she would ruin his grandson's life. She couldn't do that to him so she wrote JG a note and then she left with us."

"So she had no idea—"

"That JG had been poisoned? No. By the next morning, by the time she was forcing me to get up, she'd already realized she was wrong to leave as she had. She said she was going to return to London at the first opportunity because it wasn't fair to cut JG out of the decision of having a life together or not based on what that hateful old man had said and might do."

Jane nodded.

"She made me tell her exactly what happened the night before. Not only then but at earlier times when I thought I saw or heard something incriminating. It was in telling and retelling her everything that I began to see the possibility that I might have been mistaken. Terribly, horribly mistaken. And if I had been, I might have driven him into the arms of Miss St. Clair, and there would be no one to blame but myself. I didn't know which was worse, thinking I'd been betrayed or that I had done the betraying without meaning to."

"Oh, dear."

"I tried to write to him, but I couldn't find the words. I had no appetite. Either I could not sleep or I slept too much. I was quite the sight. When Nigel showed up, I swooned for the first time in my life. He didn't know what to make of it." She leaned in to confide, "I thought I was hallucinating him."

Jane gave her a sad smile.

"We made up, of course."

Jane's smile broadened. "I knew that part."

"My point in all this is that I made myself unwell enough that my monthly occurrence was irregular from then on."

"I see."

"It was around Christmas time last year that I thought, I hoped, I was with child. But I wasn't. It was so disappointing. I remember that monthly was so dreadful, unlike I had experienced before, it made me feel like I was being punished for even thinking I was with child. I know that doesn't make any sense."

"No, it doesn't," Jane said tenderly. "But we can get odd thoughts in our mind that are difficult to shake."

"I have been asked about the timing of my last menstruation by the doctor, and I tried to determine when it was. I only recall having one in the spring."

"What month was it?"

"April. It was over by the time of Ada's wedding, which I was glad for."

"That was the end of April," Jane mused.

"But they had been so irregular," Alice reiterated. "I didn't *feel* with child, I didn't know for certain until June, I would say."

"Meaning you felt ill at that time?" Jane inquired.

"Very. And tired beyond reason."

"It's not uncommon for those symptoms to occur in the third and fourth month rather than the first few. Meaning you might be ready to have this child sooner than you thought."

Alice thought about it. If that was true, she had been very wrong to have travelled so far and so late in the year. "I would very much like to meet Astrid."

"She's a dear girl," Jane said reassuringly. "You'll be glad to know her."

Chapter Fifteen

Astrid was twenty, soft spoken, and gentle natured. She was patient and affectionate with the children. Jane had frequently observed her tutoring and playing with the children, but she had never before seen her in the role of midwife. That's what occurred to her as she led the way to Alice's room.

Astrid's elder sister, Emilia Wahl, was twenty-six, more forthright and yet markedly reserved. Life had been less than fair or kind to her. Jane knew this because Emilia had become a friend.

The two of them communicated about everything from menus to the children's education to the plants in the greenhouse. Jane was grateful to have her as a housekeeper and a companion, and Emilia was thankful to have a home for herself, her children, and her sister at Manoria.

Jane could not claim she knew Astrid well. She liked her, but their paths only crossed when the children were involved. She reached the door to Alice and Nigel's room and knocked.

Alice quickly opened it. She had undressed and put on a wrapper. She seemed vulnerable, and it made Jane feel self-conscious and uncomfortable on Alice's behalf. After introductions, Jane started to take her leave, but Alice spoke up, preferring her to stay, so she stood near the door ready to either help or go, as needed.

"Tell me how and what you're feeling," Astrid said, gesturing to her own body. She and Alice stood facing one another in the center of the room.

"There is some aching," Alice said, placing her hands at the base of her belly bulge.

"Dull aching?"

Alice nodded. "Yes. Mostly."

"What about your breathing? Has there been a change in your ease of breathing?"

Alice looked surprised. "Yes. Just the last day or so. How did you know?"

"That is what happens. The baby has dropped a bit lower in preparation for the birth. That's why the ache is lower, while the pressure up high, against the lungs, is less."

Alice blinked. "The baby is readying itself for birth? And it's normal?"

Astrid smiled. "Yes. To both. Do you have much discomfort in your low back?"

Alice shook her head. "No more than I have had. Or not much more."

"Good. That probably means the child is in the ideal position."

"What is the ideal position?"

"His or her head is down and facing me. When the baby faces the other way, we call that back-to-back, and it makes for a great deal of discomfort in the mother's lower back." She paused. "You said dull aching mostly. Are you experiencing abdominal cramping?"

"Some. Yes."

"How often?"

Alice shook her head. "A few times an hour, I suppose."

"And how long do they last?"

Alice thought about it. "Not long, really. I haven't paid that much attention."

"Begin making a note of when they occur and how long they last. Alright?"

Alice nodded.

"When did they begin?"

"Last afternoon. No, last evening, but they weren't regular. I was woken twice in the night with pain, though."

Astrid wrinkled her nose sympathetically. "It's nearly impossible to get comfortable, isn't it?"

"Yes. It is. I expected that. I have two elder sisters and five nieces and nephews."

"Tell me about them as we walk a bit." As the two of them paced the floor and Alice described her sisters and nieces and nephews, Astrid watched Alice's form.

Alice suddenly stopped and turned to Astrid. "I passed blood a few days ago," she said.

Astrid nodded. "That's common."

"It is?"

"Yes. I believe you are close to giving birth. I cannot say how close unless I examine you, but that is up to you. The doctor can be fetched at any point in time."

"But how is bleeding normal?"

"It was a bit of blood, yes? Not a flow."

Alice nodded.

"The bottom of the womb has a natural seal for the baby's protection," Astrid explained. "When the baby drops, preparing itself for birth, that seal is pushed out. Some women do not notice it at all. Others see it as a brownish discharge or a bit of blood. All are perfectly normal."

"I wish the doctor had said so. He only said everything looked fine and I wasn't to worry."

"He wasn't wrong, just not as forthcoming as he might have been."

Jane bit back a smile.

"Doctor Setterfield is a fine man," Astrid continued. "And a very good physician but he is rather awkward with ladies. I've assisted him with a birth a time or two."

Alice sighed. "You cannot know how you have relieved my mind."

"I'm glad."

"I would like you to examine me."

"Then I shall. You can either lie down or sit down with your legs spread apart and I'll determine if dilation has begun. Do you know what that is?"

"I'm not certain."

"The lowest part of the womb is the cervix. It opens, widens, in childbirth. Two things will allow the baby to be born. The contractions, the pains—"

"I know what that is," Alice interjected teasingly.

"And the dilation of the cervix, so the baby can pass through."

That it was stated in such a straightforward, unembarrassed manner helped immeasurably. Jane was impressed.

"Have you attended many births?" Alice asked.

"Oh, yes. I helped my mother from a young age. When she became ill, I took over more and more while she supervised. At the end, I was on my own."

"I'm sorry for your loss."

"Thank you. I miss her, but she's still with me. I feel her steadiness when I need it. Are you ready?"

"Yes." Alice toddled over to the bed, and Astrid followed. Alice took a breath and exhaled before she opened her wrapper and sat. Astrid knelt in front of her. "Scoot forward to the very edge," she coaxed. "That's it." She eased Alice's legs apart. "Now I'm going to reach in and feel what's happening, which may be nothing at all yet. Alright?"

Alice nodded tightly. Her tension was obvious.

"It will be uncomfortable, but not painful."

Jane chewed on her bottom lip and looked away. She'd never been through the examination of another woman, but she admired Astrid's calm, professional manner. She heard Alice draw in a sharp breath.

"It's not much yet, but it's begun," Astrid announced a moment later.

Alice pulled her legs and her wrapper back together. "Shall I lie down?"

"No. It could be hours, or it could be days, especially with a first birth." She rose and walked to the washstand to clean her hands. "You should do whatever you can to distract yourself. Sew, play cards. Walk. Walking is good. A warm bath can feel wonderful. Just be sure to get assistance getting in and out of the tub."

"Hours or days," Alice repeated. "I thought I had a month, still."

Astrid turned back to her as she dried her hands. "I have a few pointers that may help. When you stand, make certain your shoulders are above your hips. Pregnant women tend to push their bellies out."

Alice stood and then adjusted herself. "I didn't realize I was doing that."

"Because it's so natural a thing," Astrid said with a shrug. "Now, straighten your feet. It's also natural to have them turned out in late pregnancy."

Alice laughed but did it. "I am so glad you're here."

Jane beamed a smile at Astrid. She, too, was glad. Exceedingly glad.

~~~

At dinner, everyone could see how buoyant Alice felt after having the housekeeper's sister examine her. Alice had been reassured. She appeared to be prepared for the coming birth.

Tomorrow, most the guests were departing. Alexandria was taking Arthur and Charlotte in her carriage. They would lead the caravan followed by Dab and Theo, and Hugh and Jonathan.

The evening was one of heartfelt conversations. The time spent at Manoria had been a beginning of a few new friendships and a deepening of others. A momentous event was imminent, and they all felt a shifting in their own lives. Marriages, children, the building of families loomed on the horizon. Every holiday going forward would have new faces and there would be new roles to play.

Alice was experiencing occasional pains. It was apparent by a tightening on her face and the fact that she would get up and pace, one hand pressed to her back. Everyone kept a discreet eye on her, and Jocelyn made a careful note of the timing.

At eight o'clock, Jane excused herself to say goodnight to Arthur. He was in bed, having been bathed and tucked in. Only the collar of his white cotton nightgown showed above the blankets. Jane sat beside him and leaned down to kiss his forehead. "Are you excited about the trip?"

Arthur nodded. "I wish you were going."

"But this can be your special time with Grandmother and Grandfather, and Grammy and Gramps and Aunt Tess and Uncle Morgan and Granny Bea, and all of them. I'll be there before long." She smoothed his hair and took inventory of every feature on his beautiful, sleepy face. "I've packed some books and toys to make the ride go faster."

"I'm glad Miss Charlotte is riding with us."

"So am I." She leaned forward and kissed him again, breathing in his scent. "I love you."

"I love you, too, Mamma."

Jane left the room and closed the door. She couldn't imagine her life without Arthur, and she wanted another child. Her fingers dropped to her abdomen and pressed lightly. She so wanted another baby.

~~~

Astrid did not know who had invited Zander to dine with them that evening, but it felt like a conspiracy that her sister had taken part in. The maids were besotted with him. Even Mrs. Duffy was enamored by his boyish charm and good looks.

The only thing Astrid could say in his defense was that he wasn't flirting back with the maids. He wasn't flirting with anyone except for her, despite the fact she'd made it clear she was not interested. There was no point in being interested when he was leaving tomorrow.

"You should give Zander a tour," Duffy said to her when the meal was over.

Astrid gave her a cool look. "A tour of what?"

"Well, down here, a'course. Most interesting rooms in the house, if you ask me."

Astrid turned to Zander, skewering him with a dower expression. "Are you enthralled by kitchens and such?"

"I am," he replied with enthusiasm. "A tour would be grand."

"I'll show you," Georgia spoke up.

"Go check on them upstairs," Duffy ordered her. "Both of you," she said to Clarice.

The maids went. Resentfully.

Astrid leaned back in her chair as she crossed her arms. "You saw the main kitchen," Astrid said to Zander. "This is our dining hall."

He nodded. "I thought it might be."

"The scullery and laundry are on that side and on the other are larders, salting room and the still room. Downstairs is the wine cellar."

"And the water cistern," Emilia said. "Personally, I find that fascinating."

"As would I," Zander agreed. "Would you show me?" he asked Astrid.

All eyes were on her.

"It's cold down there," she replied stiffly. "But if you wish."

"I do, Miss Astrid. But only if you don't mind. If you do, I suppose I could go on my own."

"It's only that I wouldn't like to delay you," she said tartly. "You probably ought to get your rest, leaving tomorrow and all."

"I don't need that much sleep. Never have."

She scooted her chair back and rose, acutely aware of being this evening's entertainment. She gestured him forward and then walked out with her head held high and her cheeks steadily heating. A conspiracy amongst her own kith and kin. That's what this was.

Zander glanced in the rooms they passed and asked a few questions, which she answered curtly. At the door to the cellar, she lit a taper before handing it to him. She then took one for herself, held the wick to his and lit it, glancing up to find his gaze on her. There was not a smirk in sight. In fact, his expression was serious and tender.

Tosh! What was she going on about? He was leaving in the morning. Lifting her skirt, she made her way down the steps carefully. "The wine cellar is that way, the cistern this way." She walked on, halting at the entrance to the water cistern.

To be fair, it was a fascinating place, almost otherworldly. A murky, cavernous, subterranean world. The walls were smooth sandstone, as was the cistern. It was some ten feet in diameter. The damp air smelled of wet earth, and the sound of dripping was constant except for during heavy rains when there was more of a hiss from the stronger flow.

"Never seen the like," he marveled. His voice was amplified before it echoed back. He laughed with wonder.

He was delightful without even trying. It was his friendly, curious open nature.

He stepped further into the space. "Rainwater must funnel from the roof," he said as his finger traced a line in the air along the pipe. "Down through there."

There was a pressing muteness to the room that felt intimate, as if their very presence was amplified. Beyond the illumination of their candles were glimmers here and there. Darkness swallowed the rest of it.

He moved closer and squatted to study valves and the pump. "I would guess there's some sort of filtering layer before it comes out here."

The light of his candle bouncing off the wall backlit his form. The light from hers, shone on his back and shoulder and leg. Her gaze ought to have been more contained, but who was to know? "That's what I was told," she replied. "Layers of rocks and sand. Which does not sound particularly filtering—"

He stood and nodded before turning to her. "Except with years and years and gallons upon gallons. It's fascinating, alright."

"And chilly. Shall we?"

"Astrid—"

She had already turned to go, but reluctantly turned back to him. "Yes?"

"I have something to ask you. Would you mind if I come back?"

Back to the cistern? She was confused. "Come back?"

"Here. Would you mind if I came back here? To live. To work."

Her breath caught. "In the village, you mean?" She shrugged and looked away. "Why would I mind? But—"

"No, I mean here. Manoria."

She jerked her head toward him so quickly, a muscle in the back of her neck burned.

"Reg put in a good word for me and, turns out, Lord Larrowford is probably going to get a new carriage that requires a driver. There's also plenty of work around here to do besides the occasional driving."

"You're saying … you spoke to Lord Larrowford?"

"Aye." He smiled and started toward her. "I'll tell you what's astonishing is how nice they all are. I met a lot of rich pricks in my day." He broke off with a grimace. "Beggin' your pardon. Arrogant and not nice, I meant. They've got money and titles, so they think they're worlds better than you. I've met my share of poor and dastardly, too. Cruel, heartless, they'd sooner stick you then have you in their way. But these are good people. I'd be honored to work for any of them."

She was too overwhelmed to form an intelligent reply. Her heart was hammering in an unnatural and unhealthy manner. "Let's go up," she said. "It's cold." She turned and walked on, trying to even out her breathing. Her shivering could be explained by the chill, but the fact that she was completely breathless would give her away. She reached the steps and hoisted her skirt. "Lord Larrowford has agreed to hire you?" she asked as she went up.

"Aye."

The reached the ground floor and she made a business of blowing out her candle and setting it down.

"I want to come back," he declared earnestly. He blew out his candle. "But I won't if you don't want me to." He handed her the taper.

She reached out for it and their hands touched. She took it, set it aside and then looked back at him. "Why would I mind?" she asked warily.

"I suppose you'd mind if you don't want me pursuing you."

Thank goodness for the dim lighting. Hopefully he could not tell the extent of her blushing. Her cheeks were aflame. "Good gracious," she exclaimed. "We've just met. You cannot possibly know that you'd want to pursue me."

"I can know that. I do know that. I'd get down on one knee right now if it wouldn't send you scuttering away in a blind panic."

Her jaw nearly dropped. It took a moment to draw a breath to respond. "To answer your question, Mister McShane, I would not object to your return, but I will not stand here and listen to such silly talk." She looked down and smoothed her skirt. "I can see you doing well here. Liking it. We all like it." Why were the words so cursedly difficult to come out with?

She chanced a glance at him and saw him smiling joyously. She fixed him with a stern look. "You do not need to don a victorious expression, sir. I have said nothing that would make you feel … victorious."

"And yet I do," he said softly. "Miss Cayley."

She chewed on the end of her tongue to hopefully ward off the tears that beckoned, but then she realized she could not restrain a smile from breaking through, so she marched on.

He took hold of her arm, halting her. "I—"

She turned back.

"I leave in the morning. Taking Lord and Lady Sonden back."

"I know."

"Then I'll return with Lord and Lady Larrowford either in their new carriage, if he gets one, or in the old."

"I'm pleased to hear there's a plan." She'd stammered the last of it, which heightened her discomfiture.

"Oh, there's a plan," he said suggestively enough that she answered with a censorious look that made him laugh.

He was impossible! She would likely never get her way or win an argument with him because he would melt her ire away with his damned Irish charm.

"My last question for the evening is this," he said. "May I kiss you … to keep me warm on the long drive back?"

"You certainly may not."

His gaze caressed her face. "May I kiss your cheek?"

She hesitated. "I … I think not."

"Then your hand. May I kiss your hand, Miss Cayley?"

She swallowed. "Fine." She held out her hand and he embraced it in both of his before slowly lifting it to his lips. His gaze shifted to hers as his lips caressed the back of her hand. Damnation! She couldn't breathe!

"Thank you," he said softly before releasing it. "I don't suppose you'd want to kiss me?"

She wasn't completely successful at restraining her smile this time, so she took the lead again. Her heart was soaring! Positively soaring!

Chapter Sixteen

Charlotte, Alexandria, and Arthur rode in Lord and Lady Carrick's second-best carriage, a lavish conveyance, with the ladies' feet perched on a brass footwarmer, which helped immeasurably. Arthur's feet didn't reach. The seats were well padded, and heavy lap blankets helped allay the cold. Alexandria and Arthur sat next to one another on the forward-facing seat while Charlotte faced them.

The curtains in the windows had been tied at the bottom, so Charlotte watched the snow as they rode. Her heart felt as light as the softly falling wisps. Hugh was two carriages behind them, although they would soon outpace his as well as Dab's since four horses pulled this vehicle.

Hugh.

What an astonishing few days it had been. Would her parents guess what had occurred simply by looking at her?

"You're in love with him, aren't you?" Alexandria asked.

Charlotte looked at her sharply, but no response rushed to her rescue. Yes, she was in love with him, but it wasn't something she would declare here and now.

"He feels the same for you," Alexandria added smugly. "I've seen it for a while. I'm truly glad for you."

"Thank you," Charlotte uttered, although it came out sounding more like a question than she'd intended.

"You two are well suited," Alexandria stated. "You're both intelligent and, well ... nice."

Charlotte grinned. "Thank you." This time there was no question mark involved. It may have been tepid praise, but from Alexandria, Charlotte would take it in the spirit in which it was intended. Which was mostly well-meaning with a dash of superiority that came so naturally, the younger woman might not even be aware of it. She was frequently *un*self-aware.

"You were so good at that rhyming game. I was not very good at it."

"What rhyming game?" Arthur asked.

Alexandria shifted to face her nephew. "The person who starts, asks a question to the next person who must answer it with a rhyme before saying something to the next in line."

"For example," Charlotte said, "I might ask Alexandria, 'Are you mad?'"

"No, I am glad," Alexandria replied. "You see?"

Arthur nodded. "Let's play!"

"Alright," Alexandria said. "How old are you?" she asked Arthur.

"I'm twenty-two," he replied. "How old are you?" he asked Charlotte.

Charlotte shook her head. "We forgot to say. You can't repeat the same question. Try again with a new question."

He thought about it. "Do you like playing in the snow?"

"The answer is absolutely no!" She looked at Alexandria. "Am I dressed warmly enough for that?"

"You're wearing a coat and a hat." Alexandria replied choppily. Then she giggled, pleased with herself. "Are you excited to see your grandmother and grandfather?"

Arthur frowned for a moment, and then replied, "Why else would I bother?"

The ladies laughed and Charlotte clapped. "Excellent! You are good at this game."

~~~

Dab and Theo rode in their new landau, acquired because the carriage was enclosed. Dab had hired a driver for the trip, a particularly congenial man, and had been considering employing him on a permanent basis until he learned that Zander MacShane planned to return to Manoria. Apparently, he'd fallen for the housekeeper's sister. Yet more proof of Manoria's enchantment.

115

It was a quiet sniff and a quick swipe of her eye that made Dab realize Theo was feeling emotional. "What is it?" he asked. "What's wrong?"

She shook her head. "Nothing's wrong."

"Then why are you crying?"

"I'm not really crying. Oh, I don't know. No reason, really." She shrugged and then fumbled for her handkerchief which she used to dab at her eyes and nose. "I'm so happy for Alice," she continued in a thick voice. "Soon, she'll have the baby. She was so beautiful. Don't you think she was beautiful?"

He took hold of her hand. "Yes, I do."

"Mothers-to-be are so beautiful," she said wistfully.

"Yes, they are," he agreed.

He kissed her cheek and she laughed and wiped at her nose again. "That was probably a bit wetter than you prefer."

"Not at all."

~~~

"You would be more comfortable riding up there," Hugh reminded Jonathan since they had no cabin to keep the air off them and the snow from occasionally flying in at them. The hood was in place, of course, and, fortunately, the wind was minimal. "Not to mention you'd get there faster." They were only caravanning to a point since both conveyances in front of them were newer, faster, and had more horses to pull them. Hugh only had one, and the old mare was reliable, but not impressive.

"Do I not look tough enough to take the elements? Don't worry about me. Apparently, I'm tougher than I look." He paused before adding, "I've gone a few rounds with Gentleman Jackson, you know."

"Really," Hugh said drolly. "I don't think you'd mentioned that."

Jonathan chuckled. "Strange, isn't it? The first of us to become a father. If it's a boy, he'll be the first son of a son of a baron."

Hugh grinned. "Do you care to make a small wager on it being a boy or girl?"

"Why? Did Alice say something I missed?"

"No."

"Did Nigel?"

"No. No one has any idea of the baby's gender, as far as I know."

"If there's to be a wager, I have to give it some thought. You know I feel strongly about winning."

Hugh laughed. "Well, you've got a fifty-fifty shot." He glanced at Jonathan. "How did you get here, by the way?"

"The usual way. My mother and father. Arriving eight minutes later than—"

"Amusing. I meant to Manoria."

"Ah. Lakely and I rode to Merton Park with Ada and Harrison in the Bower's carriage." He paused. "Bankers must do well."

Hugh grunted. "Most especially when their family owns the bank."

"True. Then Monty joined the family later, and then she and Lakely and I came to Manoria. Monty and Lakely returned to the city before you arrived for some event they wanted to attend."

"I'm sorry I missed them."

Jonathan shrugged. "Well, I hate to tell you, but they said if Hugh is coming, we are going."

Hugh laughed.

A puff of wind blew snow at them, and Jonathan grabbed at it. He opened his glove and smiled down at the few flakes. "See? You can't do that inside a cabin."

Jonathan could almost always be relied on to see the positive, as well as to bring flasks.

"I'm going to say the baby is ... a boy," Jonathan announced.

Hugh gave a single nod. "I'll say a girl."

"What's the wager? A pound? A shilling?"

Hugh scoffed. "Who has a shilling?"

"A silver penny it is, then. Or should we make it a farthing? Poor beggar, you."

Hugh gave him a look. "Keep in mind that if I boot you off, you're walking back to the city. Unless you can bellow loudly enough for the others to hear."

Jonathan gave a dramatic shiver. "Frightening. So tell me about Miss Charlotte Richards. Oh, and what happened with her dolt of a cousin? What a bore he was."

Before Hugh could reply, Jonathan elbowed him.

"By the way, I approve. I liked her from the moment I met her. I think she's marvelous."

Hugh couldn't help his smile. "So do I."

"Did I ever tell you that she and I were largely responsible for Joel and Jane getting together?"

"Yes, but wasn't it my turn to talk?"

Jonathan guffawed. "The floor is yours, man!"

Chapter Seventeen

Jane woke and sat up abruptly at the sound of a knock on their bedroom door.

Joel stirred. "You think it's Alice?"

Jane had already sprung up and was reaching for her robe. "I think it's about Alice." She threw on her robe and hurried to the door. She opened it see Jocelyn in her nightclothes, looking frantic.

"I am so sorry to wake you," Jocelyn apologized quietly.

"Don't be silly," Jane chided. "What's happening?"

"We need Astrid. Alice is shaking all over. She can't stop."

Jane stepped out in the hall and closed the door. "I'll get her." Jocelyn nodded and then rushed to get back to Alice, her robe fluttering behind her. Jane went in the other direction.

The entrance hall was pitch dark except for embers flickering in the hearth, and a long, widening strip of silver-white moonlight. The bare floor was cold. She should have stuck slippers on her feet. She stepped into the east wing and counted the doors as she passed them. The schoolroom was in the east wing as were a dozen bedchambers. There had been sixteen bedrooms, each large enough for either two narrow beds or a double bed, plus a bedside table, corner nightstand and either a narrow wardrobe or a chest of drawers. In the summer, they had enlarged some of the rooms and updated them all.

There hadn't been a project at Manoria that Jane had not enjoyed, but the work in the east wing had been particularly meaningful. They had a wonderful staff and she wanted them to be happy there.

She stopped at Astrid's door and knocked lightly. Hopefully, she wouldn't disturb anyone else. She heard movement from within before the door opened revealing a sleep disheveled Astrid. Her thick braid lay over her shoulder. With her high-necked nightgown and sleepy eyes, she looked young and innocent.

"It's Alice," Jane said. "Jocelyn says she is shaking and cannot stop."

"Getting close, then," Astrid returned quietly in a low, slightly husky voice. "I'll be right there."

What a good thing it was that she was amongst them. "I'll make sure tea and food will be on the way."

"I'll let Emilia know," Astrid said with a shake of her head. "She can alert the others."

Jane nodded and left. As she crossed back through the main hall, the clock began striking. It was four a.m. She smiled from the certainty that the baby would arrive that day. Most likely the first child born at Manoria.

Nigel stood in the corridor in his nightclothes and robe, holding a bundle of his clothing and shoes. Jane had never seen him looking so nervous. She fought a tendency to smile at the sight. Instead, she gave him a reassuring nod. "Try not to worry," she urged. "It is very likely to be hours yet."

"I feel so helpless," he admitted.

"I know, but she will be surrounded with care and love." She heard quiet footsteps behind her and turned to see Joel coming toward them. He had dressed.

Joel grinned at Nigel. "I won't claim that's not a good look on you, but are you planning to remain in your nightclothes all day?"

The ribbing was precisely what Nigel needed.

"Be gentle with him," Jane teased her husband before slipping into the room.

Alice sat on the bed and Jocelyn was beside her with an arm around her. Their heads were pressed together, and Alice's eyes were squeezed shut. She was wrapped in a blanket and being gently swayed as Jocelyn hummed.

As Jane went toward them, she could see Alice shaking. "Astrid will be here soon," she said soothingly. She squatted and stroked Alice's arm. "The trembling is normal."

Alice opened her eyes. "She said so?"

"Yes."

Alice breathed a sigh of relief.

Jocelyn kissed her sister's head. "Everything will be fine."

When Astrid arrived with her basket of birthing necessities, including a worn leather bag on top, Jane left to get dressed. It wasn't until she was fumbling to fasten the buttons on her gown that she realized she was trembling. She had never been present at any birth except her own, and that seemed like a lifetime ago.

When she returned, Astrid and Jocelyn had Alice braced between them as they walked the length of the floor. Alice was obviously in pain or at least severe discomfort.

"Don't hold your breath," Astrid reminded her. "When a pain begins, suck in a breath and then blow it out or sing it out or moan it out."

When the next pain hit, they stopped, and Alice chose a keening combination of the three.

"Good," Astrid praised.

The pain subsided and they started in motion again.

"I'm here for whatever you need," Jane said.

Astrid acknowledged her with a nod.

"I wish we could all divvy up the pain for you," Jocelyn said to her sister.

"Be careful," Alice warned. "I would let you."

"Whenever you're ready," Astrid said. "I'll check your progress. There's no hurry."

"I'm ready!"

"Alright, then. Come and sit on the edge of the bed. Jocelyn, sit behind her and let her lean against you. You may need to hold one of her legs. Jane, please come on her other side. You can hold her hand and I'll need you to support the other leg."

Never before had Astrid called her Jane. It was always a respectful Lady Larrowford. But the playing field had changed, and Jane admired her firm, calm direction. The three got in place. Astrid squatted on the floor, hoisted up Alice's gown and moved her knees up and apart. Jocelyn supported one and Jane the other. Alice stared at the ceiling as Astrid checked her. Jane watched Alice's face and her breathing.

"You are well on your way," Astrid said a moment later, as she rose. "Not quite halfway there yet, but it's a very good start."

Alice's legs were eased back down. "I wish it were finished already."

Astrid got up to wash her hands. "I understand. You and every other woman who goes through childbirth."

"Poor Nigel," Jane said lightly. "He looked so lost and frightened."

"Yes," Alice said soberly. "Poor Nigel."

The ladies all laughed until Alice experienced another pain. "Breathe," Jocelyn coaxed.

To support her, they all blew out noisy breaths in concert.

Astrid consulted her pocket watch. "Contractions right at five minutes, lasting thirty seconds. That's good."

"I would like to lie down and rest," Alice said.

The others busied themselves arranging the covers and pillows and helping Alice into bed. She was positioned on her side.

A quiet knock proceeded Duffy who carried in a large, filled tray. "I hear there's to be a new guest in attendance," the cook said with a twinkle in her eye.

"Hopefully soon," Alice replied.

Duffy nodded. "I hope so for your sake, love. We'll be sending prayers your way."

"Thank you," Alice replied with a weak smile.

"Mrs. Duffy," Jane spoke up. "Will this be the first birth at Manoria?"

The cook thought about it. "I believe it will be. I can't think who else might have had a child here." She smiled. "The first of many, I hope. A place like this is better with children. All this space is meant to be filled with the laughter and mischief and learnin' of little ones."

Jocelyn smiled warmly and nodded.

"Ring if you need anything at all," Duffy said. "One of the girls is bringing hot water and we'll keep it coming."

As Duffy left, Alice moaned quietly and buried her face into the pillow panting out a breath.

Astrid consulted her watch again.

Jocelyn offered to fix tea for everyone, but Alice declined, and Jane and Astrid went to get their own. There were buttered crumpets and scones and sausages. Clotted cream and marmalade. The tea was strong, but fresh and delicious.

As the scent reached her, Alice agreed to have some.

The food warmed and strengthened everyone.

"What was Arthur's birth like?" Jocelyn asked Jane. "Do you think about it much once it's over?"

"No. From the moment they are born, you're consumed with them. My memories of the birth are … patchy."

"It's much like any pain, really," Astrid interjected. "When you think back on it, you remember it hurt. You remember feeling it, but you don't re-experience it."

Jocelyn nodded. "That's what our eldest sister said."

"Stop trying to cheer me up," Alice said to Jocelyn, but there was humor in it.

Jocelyn batted her eyes. "Who, me?"

~~~

It was past noon and Alice was pacing again when her water broke in what felt a strange, warm gush that shocked her, despite knowing it would happen at some point. What a completely bizarre sensation! It felt like so much fluid. It was nothing like urinating on herself which is what she'd secretly expected.

Her gown was whisked away and replaced with a dry one. She was helped back to bed and her progress was checked again.

"What is it?" Alice asked breathlessly. "Is it almost over?"

"There's been significant progress," Astrid replied reassuringly.

Alice moaned. Progress? Given a choice, she would have chosen not to do this anymore. The pains were so severe, she'd been sick to her stomach. The intensity of them made the rest of the world small and far away. There was nothing but that room, that moment and that pain. Everyone and everything was outside of the circle of it. At the center was just her. And the pain.

Jocelyn had left the room, probably to report. Where was Nigel and what was he doing and thinking? He was probably frantic.

Good!

Astrid once again applied grease to Alice's most private areas to help avoid tearing. What a dreadful thought that was. Privacy had ceased to exist, but Alice did not care. She just wanted the birth over with. After Astrid completed her ministration, Alice was made as comfortable as possible. She closed her eyes and drifted. Slowly, she became aware of the conversation around her.

"—so glad you're here," Jane was saying. "But you have a gift as a midwife. I do not want your talent wasted, although you're wonderful with the children."

"The villagers know where I am," Astrid replied. "I will gladly help anyone who requests it, but I love being here. It's been nothing short of a blessing for us." There was a pause before she added, "I know Emilia told you."

There was a beat of silence before Jane replied. "Yes."

"When you have lived amidst scorn—"

Scorn?

"Without being certain of having enough food for your family or money for the rent." She paused. "The safety and acceptance here are priceless. I don't wish to be anywhere else."

"I am glad to hear it, but would you enjoy coming to the city with us sometime? Perhaps for the season?"

Astrid clucked her tongue. "My sister," she complained. "I know she means well, but—"

A contraction snatched hold again. Astrid was immediately there with her hands around Alice's abdomen to feel the movement. Alice panted and then moaned.

"Good, Alice," Astrid lauded. "Very good."

When it passed, Alice felt weary enough to sleep. She closed her eyes. How long until the next one? Another contraction gripped hold. Alice got through it and another began.

"Oh," Astrid said. "This baby is getting serious about making an appearance."

Jocelyn reentered the room before the statement was finished. "How is she doing?"

Alice cried out with pain.

From the worst pain of her life to … nothing. She'd had the baby. It had gone from, "The head is right there. Push, Alice!"

to

"Stop now! I'm going to ease the shoulder out."

to

Whoosh

And the baby was out of her. It was done. Seconds later, Jocelyn and Jane were crying as Astrid cleared out the baby's mouth with her finger. The transition was dizzying. "What is it?" Alice cried.

It was Jocelyn who answered. "A girl! Ali, it's a girl!"

Astrid smiled as she handed the baby to Alice who stared at the tiny nose, barely open eyes, and pursed rosebud lips. The baby wasn't crying. "Should she be crying?" she stammered.

Astrid laughed despite the tears pooled in her eyes. "And so the mother's worry begins. You worry if they're not crying, and you worry if they're crying too much. She looks perfect. She looks happy to meet you."

Actually, the baby looked undecided. Alice uncurled a tiny fist and looked at the fingers. How astonishing! Here she was. She held her close, kissed her and breathed in her sweet scent.

"What's her name?" Jane asked as she dried her eyes. "Have you decided?"

"We had narrowed it down to a few. But looking at her—" She released a shaky breath. "Her name is Rose." The words came out thickly and then she began to cry from a surge of emotions. "Isn't she beautiful?"

"Yes!" Three voices rang out.

Alice pressed another kiss to her baby's head. She had a daughter!

~~~

"Nigel," Jane said, having stopped in the doorway of the salon.

He bolted upright as if poised to run for his life.

Jane smiled and nodded. "It's over. They are both fine."

"Thank God," he breathed.

Jocelyn stepped through the door with a tightly swaddled infant.

Nigel stood frozen for a moment before hurriedly closing the distance between them. "So small," he breathed. "Is it a boy or a girl?"

"A girl," Jocelyn said, looking up at him with shining eyes.

Nigel exhaled as he smiled. "A girl. How's Alice?"

"She is exhausted," Jocelyn replied. "But happy and relieved." She paused before adding, "Rose."

Nigel's smiled widened. "Rose. Yes, that's perfect." Jocelyn prepared to hand the babe over causing Nigel's smile to vanish. "*Uhh,* but what if—"

"You won't drop her," Jane soothed as she moved to his side. Joel had also come closer to see the baby. Jane linked her arm through her husband's and hugged it.

"Remarkable," Joel said under his breath.

Jocelyn placed the baby in Nigel's arms. It looked as though he'd stopped breathing.

"Breathe, brother-in-law," Jocelyn teased. "It's important to breathe."

"Then blow out a noisy breath, if you need to," Jane said. She and Jaus chuckled at the jest he did not follow.

Nigel's breath was released, but as a contented sigh. "We have a daughter," he marveled.

Joel patted his back. "Congratulations, my friend. She is beautiful."

Nigel kissed his child. "A daughter," he whispered.

Chapter Eighteen

After enduring the expulsion of the afterbirth, Alice was washed, helped into a dressing robe, and settled back onto clean bedclothes. She was shaking again, this time from aftermath of exertion. She was so fatigued, she felt stunned senseless.

She watched Astrid as she went about cleaning up the mess, shoving soiled items into a basket, and wiping up the floor. "Why did you live with scorn, if I may ask. I don't wish to be intrusive. I heard you talking earlier."

Astrid straightened, having finished her chores. "It wasn't me it was directed at. It was my sister. Although no individual in a family can be singled out for persecution without the rest feeling it, too."

Alice was baffled. Emilia Wahl was a kind, young widow with two children. What could there possibly be to scorn?

Astrid went to wash her hands a final time. "Are you hungry?" she asked.

Alice had been hungry earlier. In fact, ravenous, but she wasn't at the moment. "No."

Astrid came and sat next to her in the chair. "When Emilia was thirteen, she was offered a position as a tweeny in a fine home in Down Hatherley. It was a good opportunity. Her friend Mabel Delaney was the other tweeny and, naturally, that added to the appeal for her. Of course, I didn't want her to go. She was my constant companion. But she had no tolerance for … let's just say the sight and sounds that are the companions of a midwife."

Alice nodded, understanding that meant pain and blood and screaming. Vomit and excrement. Occasionally death.

Astrid shrugged. "We are working folk. Even as a child I understood that. Papa was a miller. The mill got passed down to him and his brothers." She paused and frowned. "To make a long story short, Emilia went into service and everything was fine for a few years until she was hurt by one of the sons of the house." She looked away and grimaced. "She came home with such bruises, and she was with child."

Alice shook her head slowly. It was pointless to say how sorry she was, but she was.

Astrid looked at her again. "She was fifteen. To make things worse, her friend Mabel turned on her. Claimed Emilia brought it on herself always trying to look pretty and with her flirtatious ways." Astrid shook her head. "Emilia was pretty, but she never had flirtatious ways."

"Of course, it wasn't her fault," Alice exclaimed. How infuriating to blame a girl, a servant, for the abuse of her employer.

There was a knock on the door that silenced them. Astrid rose and started for it. It was Emilia who entered with a filled tray. "Congratulations! I had a peek at the baby and she is perfect. I'm so happy for you."

Alice smiled back at her. "Thank you."

The housekeeper set the tray down. "Sugar and milk?"

"Please."

"Extra sugar," Astrid said.

Emilia gave her sister a wry look. "I know," she rejoined lightly. She fixed and handed the cup to Alice. "How did this one do?" she asked Alice, bobbing her head toward Astrid.

"She was superb. No one could have been better."

Mrs. Wahl nodded. "No one is better, in my opinion."

Astrid linked arms with her sister. "And you are not biased at all, are you?"

"What can I take downstairs?" Mrs. Wahl asked her.

"The bucket, please."

Mrs. Wahl fetched the bucket of dirty water and left.

Astrid took a seat again and fixed herself a cup of tea. She perused the selection of delicate sandwiches, deviled cheese, thinly sliced beef, and cream and jelly, before selecting one.

Alice felt better with each sip of the overly sweet tea and each bite of sandwich. "She stayed home then," she said carefully.

"Yes. There was certainly no going back to that place. But the scorn had begun. Not from everyone, of course, but from some. Snide comments, filthy looks. If I heard, 'no better than she ought to be,' muttered once, I heard it a hundred times. You try to ignore it, but they make sure you know it."

Alice thought back on the looks of suspicion and derision she and Jocelyn had received at some of the first balls they'd attended in the city. Those would have been nothing in comparison to having one's morality called into question. At worst, they'd been thought of as American interlopers.

"Even before Noemi was born, Emilia had rekindled her friendship with Randall Wahl. He'd always been sweet on her."

"Was he a good man?"

"Oh, yes. We loved him. We did not care for his mother, or she us, but he was unfailingly gentle and loving to Emilia and Noemi. They married before Noemi was walking, so he was her papa. And the three of them made a happy home. A few years later after my father died from a heart seizure—" Astrid had to stop and collect herself. "Losing our father would have been devastating under any circumstances, but we had no warning that the end of his life was nigh. He was fine that morning and dead by noon."

"I'm sorry."

"This is such a momentous day, Mrs. Walston. I don't want to cloud it with talk of sad events."

"It's Alice. It will always be Alice to you. I would like to know unless it bothers you or it's too private."

"You could go into the village and find out the story," Astrid replied with a shrug. "Telling it does not bother me. Honestly, it doesn't even make me terribly angry or sad anymore. After all, everything that happened brought us here."

She took a sip. "After Papa passed, my brother-in-law helped support us. You've never seen a happier man then when he learned they were having another child. He was a wonderful father. He loved those children. To know what Randall looked like, you have only to look into the face of Gabriel." She sighed. "There was an accident and he died of the injury."

Alice worried her bottom lip, perilously close to tears.

Astrid picked up another sandwich. "Randall's mother blamed Emilia. Said she was cursed. When Mamma got ill, we really did feel cursed. Not by my sister, of course."

"Of course," Alice repeated softly.

"Mister Kerr, he's the steward here, he suggested we come here. Not every master would have accepted a housekeeper with such a burdensome entourage, but Lord Larrowford did."

"You've been a blessing to them, too."

There was a knock on the door and Astrid set down her cup and rose. "Come in," she called as she started toward the basket of soiled laundry.

Nigel stepped in, holding the baby. "There is a rumor that she belongs to us," he said to his wife with shining eyes. "I came to confirm."

"I can confirm it," Alice replied in a choked sounding voice.

Astrid eased out and silently closed the door behind her.

Nigel reached Alice, handed her the baby, and then leaned in to kiss her. "How are you?"

"Sore," she admitted. "Tired." She studied her daughter's tiny, squinched up face. "I can hardly believe I'm looking at her."

"I know." He sat beside her carefully, draping an arm around her legs. "This has been the longest day. I felt so useless. Did it feel as if it lasted a month to you?"

She didn't know how to answer. At times, at long intervals, it had felt as if it would never end, but now, looking at their child, she was nothing but sore and tired and astounded and possibly dazed. "Some of the pains did last a month," she replied.

He grimaced and stroked her arm. "My poor darling."

Alice kissed the baby. "She was worth it," she said softly. The baby frowned and let out a mew, so Alice pulled open her dressing robe to try nursing the baby again. Her milk was not in yet, but the suckling helped bring it about.

"I don't know that I ever truly considered what a miracle it all is," he murmured.

Her heart squeezed to see him look away to discreetly wipe away a tear. She grabbed hold of his arm and nodded her understanding. It *was* overwhelming. They had created a life, she had carried and nurtured her, and now she was here. Their baby. Their little Rose.

~~~

In the kitchen, bottles of champagne were opened with great fanfare. Noemi and Gabriel were given cups of cider, and Joel made a toast to Alice and baby Rose. Then he toasted Astrid, and then Nigel. As glasses went up again and again, Jane looked around with a full and grateful heart at all those gathered around.

Jocelyn was seated at the table, relieved, happy and tired.

Mrs. Duffy was crying, dabbing her face furiously with her hanky.

Reedman patted the lady's back and beamed.

Emilia Wahl had an arm around her sister, as proud as can be.

Astrid looked flustered as she received accolades of praise.

The children were delighted to be part of the celebration.

Thank God, Jane thought. For the birth and the baby's health and Alice's health. And this home and her husband and her son and their life. She caught Joel's eye and had the feeling he knew exactly what she was feeling. He gave her a subtle nod and a loving smile that she returned.

Chapter Nineteen

Charlotte lay curled on her side in her own bed with their purring cat cozied up next to her. People usually found it strange that they had a cat as a pet, but the cat, or rather kitten at the time, had found and adopted them so what choice did they have except to adopt her back? She'd been named Ophelia and she'd rarely made them sorry to have her. Only when she smuggled in a small bird or a mouse as a surprise gift for them. Or for a midnight snack.

Charlotte yawned. It was so good to be home, she could have purred herself. "Hugh did not think it was strange," she murmured as she stroked Ophelia's silky black fur. "But you may have a choice to make because, one day, this won't be my home. I'll have another, which you may come to, if you wish. But I know you love it here. It's your home, too."

There was a knock on the door an instant before it opened, and Martha Richards swept inside and closed the door behind her. "Darling," she said hurrying closer.

Charlotte sat up, smiling to see her mother. Charlotte had arrived back home only minutes after her mother had left for a gathering with her friends. They kissed and her mother sat beside her. "How was your get together?"

"Oh, fine," Martha replied breezily. "The usual. But you," she said, as she reached out for her daughter's hand and squeezed it. "Look at you. I simply must hear everything. Your father couldn't wait to tell me even though I told him not to. That I'd hear it from your lips. But he just went on and on. What an eventful trek you had."

"Yes. Good and bad."

"Good and bad? It sounds more like wonderful and terrible."

"I will agree with that."

"Mister Hugh Pritchett, *hmm*?" Martha said with a gleam in her eye.

Charlotte nodded. "You'll meet him on Christmas Day."

Martha sighed happily. "Look at you all radiant. Oh, but Virgil," she said with a frown. "I am so disappointed in him."

Charlotte sobered. "So am I."

"He has always been vain and self-important and more than a little thoughtless, but I am stunned by his assumption that you would marry him." She huffed with disgust. "And I am appalled at his hostility when you refused." She paused. "Am I overstating that?"

"No."

"You never even saw Millie, then?"

"No."

Martha tsked. "All that planning you did."

"It's alright," Charlotte assured her. "I would like to have seen her and her family, but the rest of the trip was extraordinary. Mamma, I fell in love!"

"I know, my love. I can see it in your pretty face. Plus, your father blabbed it."

Charlotte laughed. Her parents were so amusing. They were the best of friends but also ridiculously competitive. "I wondered if the two of you would know just by looking at me."

"Of course, we would have. At least, I would have. So," she said, shifting to get more comfortable. "I hope you're not too desperately tired because you must start at the beginning and tell me everything!"

Chapter Twenty

Hugh was thankful beyond expression to walk in the back door of his family's home and be enveloped by warmth in every way it could be felt. It was Christmas Eve, his family was all there, he could hear their voices, and the savory scent of cooking lingered in the air.

It was toasty warm in the house, but he'd practically grown icicles on the drive, so he chose to leave his coat on for the moment. He hung up his hat, peeled off his gloves, and rubbed his hands together before continuing into the parlor, where a resounding cheer went up to see him.

Sixteen family members were crowded together, but his mother maneuvered to him with ease. He kissed her cheek and she squealed. "You are freezing!"

"I know I am."

"You're in time for dinner," Selena said as she jostled their two-year old niece.

"Thank goodness," he replied. "I am famished."

"How was it?" his father asked with a curious, but pleased expression. "You look well."

"Frozen," his brother, Thom, interjected. "But otherwise well."

"Come sit by the fire," his mother urged.

Hugh accepted. He removed his coat and sat in a chair near the fire that his sister-in-law vacated for him. She sat in her husband's place, and he went to stand behind her. It was a familiar family shuffle.

"You went all the way to Gloucester?" Bertram, his eldest brother, asked.

Hugh nodded. "Not far from there. A country estate called Manoria. It's the place Joel inherited."

"What was it like?" his mother asked.

"Like a gothic mansion," he replied to a rousing response. "I'm serious. It looked like that from the outside and … parts of the interior, as well. Not gloomy or haunted. I don't mean that. It was built a hundred years ago by someone ridiculously wealthy as a hunting lodge."

"A hunting lodge?" Thom exclaimed.

Bertram made a face. "Suppose it must be nice. Yes, I have this gothic mansion here. I use it as a hunting lodge."

"If I had any artistic talent," Hugh said. "I would sketch it for you. But it is a *home*, one that Joel and Jane have filled with love. The servants—"

That drew another spirited response.

"Yes, there were servants," he continued when the clamor died down. "But they were more like trusted friends than employees. There are children there and gaiety. We had a wonderful time."

"I have a question," his sister, Anne, said with a wicked grin. "Are you agreeable to eat with the likes of us? Are we fancy enough for you now?"

Thom nodded. "Especially after spending time in a gothic mansion, being waited on hand and foot by servants."

Hugh sniffed and examined his fingernails. "I have been thinking about that," he teased.

Everyone snickered.

"No, I am thrilled to be in your company, and that is God's honest truth."

"I'm so glad you're home," his mother said. "Safe and sound."

"Tell us more about it," Bertram spoke up. "Who was there? Any dukes or kings or such?"

"No. Just the usual cast of characters and their wives and a few others."

Selena was giving him a suspicious look.

"What?" he asked.

"You look good," she commented.

He mocked offence. "You make that sound unusual."

More laughter erupted.

His father nodded thoughtfully. "I'm going to side with your sister on this. I see a spark in you that wasn't there when you left."

Hugh took a moment to respond. "If you are looking for me to say that you were right about needing to go, you were right. I did need it. It did me more good than I can say." The last of it was said in a thick voice, and he had to take a moment because of the lump in his throat.

"Hugh?" Anne asked. "What is it?"

He smiled. "There is a lady—" He didn't get more than that out before his family erupted in delight. He nodded and laughed right along with them. At this rate, dinner would be cold by the time he explained everything, but it was wonderful to be in the bosom of his family about to tell them about the lady he had fallen in love with.

Chapter Twenty-One

December 30

The greetings, when they arrived home, were just as jubilant as Jocelyn had expected. There were hugs all around, and Aunt Julia and Granny were captivated by baby Rose. All the staff wanted a peek. Moments later, Julia pulled Jocelyn away. "JG is here," she said quietly.

Jocelyn was confused because he hadn't known they were arriving this afternoon. Then she saw the reality in her aunt's face. "His grandfather?"

Julia nodded. "He's in the upstairs parlour."

Jocelyn started for the stairs, encountering her cousin Jeremy on the way. He lifted his hand in an awkward hello and she tapped it as she passed him.

"Welcome home, cousin," he said.

"Thank you."

She knew when she saw JG that he'd heard the commotion below, but he'd waited for her. Dressed in black, he looked drawn and a bit thinner. She went to him, and they embraced. "I'm so sorry," she said brokenly.

He hugged her tighter. "I was in time."

She waited for his grip to ease before she pulled back. "When?"

"He passed away sometime in the early hours of the twenty-third."

She blinked. "That was the day Rose was born."

"Rose! How is she? How is Alice?"

Jocelyn nodded. "Both are perfectly well."

"We have a niece," he said with a smile.

"She is our fourth niece," Jocelyn replied with a loving smile.

He kissed her and pressed his forehead to hers. "I have missed you," he whispered.

"I have missed you, but I'm so glad you were with him."

He pulled back. "He slept most of the time. He was in pain and heavily medicated, but he knew I was there. He said—" he broke off and cleared his throat. "He said four final words to me at the end."

I love you, Grandson, was what Jocelyn expected. Lord Morguston had not been a tender or demonstrative man, but she hadn't doubted that he loved his only grandson. He'd made the mistake of trying to control him, but even that was out of protectiveness. Well, pride and protectiveness. His title and the estate meant everything to him.

"I was telling him I would do my best to make him proud," JG uttered. "He listened and then he smiled. 'It is yours now.' That's what he said."

She exhaled and her eyes filled. She understood. In that statement, Lord Morguston had pledged his faith in him.

He swallowed. "I think there are no words that would have meant more."

She gathered him in her arms again. She kissed his cheek and caressed the hair at the nape of his neck. She would have absorbed his pain, all his pain, if she could.

"The clocks were all stopped. The door is draped in black. Everything is muffled and—"

She pulled back.

"It feels dead," he concluded with a pained expression.

"What about the funeral?"

"It's done. It was held three days later. It was dignified and crowded. I don't know how liked he was, but he was respected."

"Yes, he was," she agreed.

"I just wanted it over."

She hated that she hadn't been there for him.

"That's why I'm here," he said. "Granny and Aunt Julia and Jeremy have been so kind. I was closer to you here. Is it terrible, do you think, to detest the shroud of mourning?"

"No."

He kissed her tenderly. "I want life. I want you. We won't have to go through with the big wedding, now. We can do it any way you wish. We can have the ceremony right here with friends and family only. They are the ones that count."

She tried to restrain her smile at first. It seemed wrong to be glad when she'd just learned his grandfather had passed. But she had never wanted the showy ceremony in the city's largest church filled with the elite she did not know. She nodded. "We'll talk about it when the time is right."

"Soon," he urged.

She nodded. "Soon."

"I just want life," he said.

From downstairs came the squeal of an infant.

"Speaking of which," she said.

"Yes! Take me to meet our fourth niece. I cannot wait to see her."

She took hold of his hand, and they left the room together.

Jane Shoup is the award-winning author of Down in the Valley, (Kensington), Knightfall, (Boroughs), An American Baroness, Ammey McKeaf, and many more. She lives in North Carolina with her husband Scott, rescue-pup, Gabby, and near her three grown daughters and their families, including five grandchildren.

Visit her website at www.janeshoup.com